STEEPED IN SUSPICION

A PEBBLE COVE TEAHOUSE MYSTERY

ERYN SCOTT

KRISTOPHERSON PRESS

Published by Kristopherson Press

www.erynscott.com

erynwrites@gmail.com

Facebook: @erynscottauthor

Sign up for my newsletter to hear about new releases and sales!

Cover by Victoria Cooper

Map by Hanna Sandvig at The Book Cover Bakery

For "Mayor" Stubbs, honorary mayor of Talkeetna, Alaska from 1997-2017.

(Photo credit: Jenni Konrad)

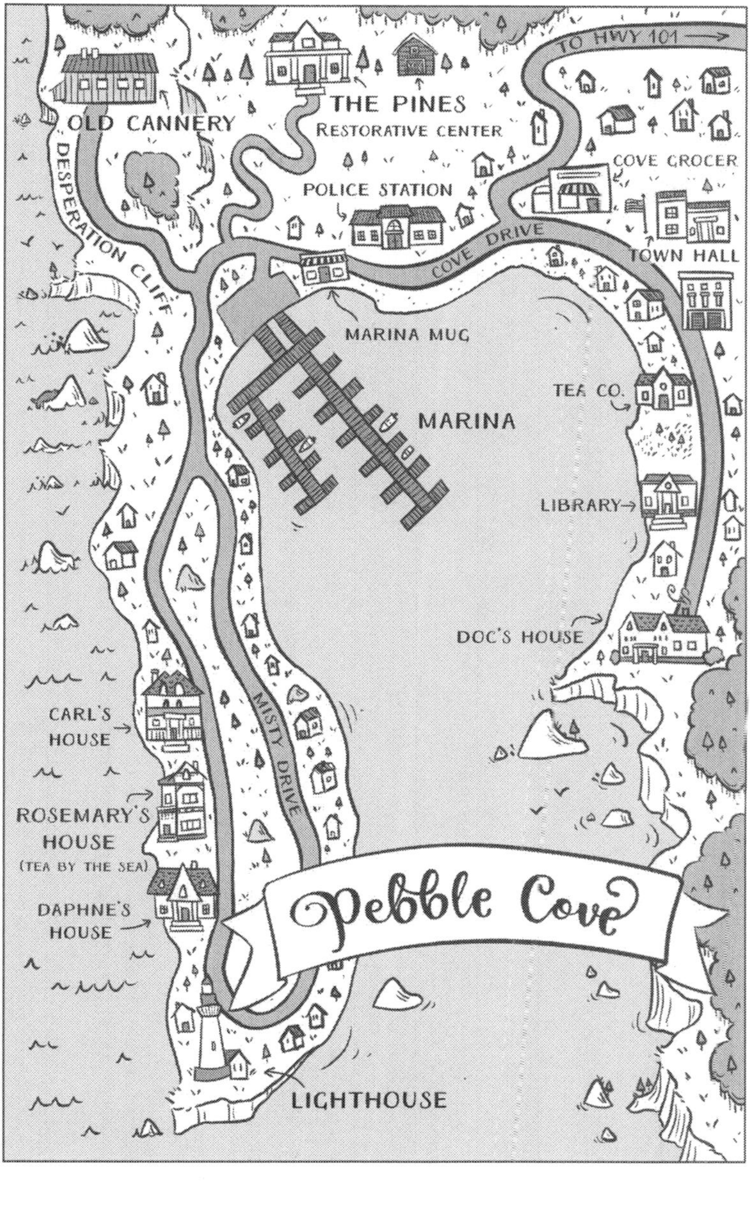
TO HWY 101
OLD CANNERY
THE PINES
RESTORATIVE CENTER
DESPERATION CLIFF
COVE GROCER
POLICE STATION
COVE DRIVE
TOWN HALL
MARINA MUG
TEA CO.
MARINA
LIBRARY
DOC'S HOUSE
MISTY DRIVE
CARL'S
HOUSE
ROSEMARY'S
HOUSE
(TEA BY THE SEA)
DAPHNE'S
HOUSE
Pebble Cove
LIGHTHOUSE

1

There was a point in my life when I thought I would never return to my grandmother's beach house in Pebble Cove.

Then again, there was also a point when I doubted I would live to see my tenth birthday and here I stood, the day after my twenty-fifth.

I approached the house trying to sort out the feelings rushing around me as palpably as the coastal winds.

Was I still mad at Grandma?

I suppose it didn't quite matter anymore. Unlike me—placing foot after foot on the stones which led up to the stately house—she would never walk this path again.

She was gone.

My fingers clutched the letter I'd received from her lawyer informing me of her passing, and how she'd left me the house and the tea shop she ran here. She'd left my mother her personal diary and a yellowed letter I knew Mom wouldn't open, but everything else, she'd bequeathed to me.

Tears threatened at the edges of my eyes, stinging in the

wind. It wasn't a surprise, I suppose; the woman was almost ninety years old. It wasn't uncommon for a person my age to lose a grandparent. The unusual part was that I hadn't spoken to my grandmother in fifteen years.

I'd never gotten up the courage to come see her. Even though I'd thought about her often, I'd still been unable to parse my mother's feud with Grandma from my own feelings. Now that she was gone, the regret of never having reached out to her felt like a kick to the gut.

I glanced back at my car wondering if it was too late to turn back, to run away. My long hair plastered itself to my face. I added *remember to tie my hair up into a bun before exiting the car* to my list of things I wished I'd done. I forgot how blustery it got here on the coast. I suppose I hadn't been here for over a decade, so it was understandable that I forgot.

The things I couldn't forget if I tried? The way the waves lapping at the shore made me whole when I hadn't even realized I was missing a thing. The soft notes of my grandmother's wind chimes, clanging as the wind brushed through them. How her gabled Victorian house had been sitting on that beach for a hundred years and would last a hundred more.

Even though I'd only spent a few summers here, I remembered, sunrise to sunset days spent on the beach exploring. After so many years, the house in Pebble Cove joined Narnia and Hogwarts in my memory: places that were so vivid, such a part of my soul, but that I'd accepted I would never physically visit. It felt eerie to be here now, filling me with as much excitement as it did unease.

I didn't know what I would do with the place. I could sell it right away, like my mom wanted me to do. The realtor said she had an offer on the table already. Or maybe it would be better to rent it out for a while and wait for the market to pick back up. Either way, I had a few days to decide before I went back to my Portland basement apartment on Monday.

Glancing down at the key in my other hand, I swallowed my doubts and walked forward.

The gray color of the paint, along with the stark white trim made the home look updated, welcoming. The front door contained half windows with designs cut in the glass, which caught the light in a diamond-like faceted way. Business hours were posted in one of the small windows. A wrought-iron hanger attached to the house held a sign over the door.

Even though the house hadn't been a tea shop back when I used to visit, my grandmother always had an affinity for herbal healing and nontraditional medications.

A pit grew in my stomach. It had been *that* very interest that had led to the fight between her and my mom.

Stepping under the sign, I shoved the key into the lock, pushing aside the memories I didn't know how to deal with right now.

The breeze fell away as I entered. I eyed the ornate rug that ran down a short hall as I pushed the door closed, cutting off the last bits of wind that attempted to follow me.

Inside, the air was cool and stagnant. The smell of tea leaves permeated the place to such a degree that I half expected the air to be tinted sepia, and for the light scent of sugar to sparkle at the edges of my vision.

I proceeded forward into the main tearoom. It didn't sparkle, but the place had a softness to it. From the smooth edges of the dark wood that lined the floors, to the wooly pillows, cushions, and blankets that sat atop chairs of every shape and size. Along one of the interior walls was a large wooden bar that appeared to have been lifted straight out of an old English pub.

From the half-dozen small tables dotting the large room and the barstools, it seemed that the tearoom was a café of sorts. But the bar also held prepackaged teas that told me Grandma sold her blends in addition to serving them.

A towering bookshelf to my left held stacked board games, card sets, and a few paperbacks. In one corner of the main room, a stack of political yard signs leaned at an angle. In another corner were baskets full of blankets and outdoor seat cushions. The house was just as beautiful inside as it was outside. The home's high ceilings and thick moldings fit in with the mental picture I conjured when I thought of Victorian-style houses.

My attention moved to my grandmother's kitchen. I

wondered if the stained-glass bird I gave her for her seventieth birthday still hung in the window over her sink.

I would've peeked inside to check … if it hadn't been for the man filling the doorway, standing in the way. I jumped, surprised to see another soul where I'd expected only nostalgia.

His dark hair was swept back off his face, and dark stubble covered his chin. From his tweed pants, suspenders, and button up, I realized I hadn't completely left the hipsters behind in Portland. His face was pulled into such a severe scowl that I was overcome with the need to make him smile.

He stopped when he spotted me, jumping a bit at the sight of me too. Then he raised his eyebrows. "This must be the granddaughter, then." The words were clipped, tired, neither inviting nor unwelcoming.

This must be the neighbor the realtor warned me might be here watering the plants.

He wasn't who I'd been expecting. For some reason, I'd pictured someone closer to my grandmother's age. This man couldn't have been much older than me, definitely not over thirty. I opened my mouth, ready to confirm that I was "the granddaughter," but before I could, he walked toward the tea bar.

"How did I not even hear you come in?" He shook his head. "Two weeks alone and I'm getting soft."

Was he staying here in addition to watering the plants? I wondered as I regarded him. He sure seemed at home, the way he walked behind the counter and began reading a newspaper sitting on the tea bar. I, on the other hand, couldn't foresee relaxing at all while this surly, sighing, suspender-wearing man was around.

I was about to ask him one of the many questions lining up in my brain when the bell on the front door jingled. The sound of footsteps followed a gust of wind down the hallway. I squeezed my eyes shut as I—all too late—realized I hadn't locked the door behind me. Between this plant-watering neighbor who seemed to have moved in, and now whoever had just let themselves inside, Pebble Cove was turning out to be a place with very few boundaries.

Glancing up at Mr. Suspenders, I caught him heave out another sigh. I couldn't hear what he muttered after that, but it sounded a lot like, "Now she's done it."

"Helloooo." The greeting bounced off the walls of the long hallway.

My shoulders tensed. I might not be as far left on the sour spectrum as Mr. Suspenders, but making small talk with people had never been one of my strengths.

My strengths were more along the lines of getting lost in a book, so much so that the world around me fell away, or clearing my throat as if I might say something but then not saying anything. I wasn't shy. I just hated being the center of attention … or even to the immediate left or right of attention. I'd had enough attention for all the wrong reasons before I even hit puberty.

Cloggy shoes clomped around the corner and broke me out of my thought bubble. I glanced up to see a middle-aged woman enter the room.

"Hi there!" she said, patting her coifed, chin-length brown hair even though it looked as if it contained enough hairspray to hold it in place through a hurricane. "I've been watching you." She flashed me a smile.

My discomfort ratcheted up a few notches at her statement.

Her smile faltered. She stepped toward me. "I mean, I'm not a stalker or anything. Just your neighbor."

"Some might say those are the same," muttered Mr. Suspenders.

My eyes widened at his curt and candid remark. I tried to gauge the woman's reaction, but she either didn't hear him, or ignored him, because she held her hand out and said, "I'm Daphne Bertraud, by the way. And you must be Rosemary."

She was watching me and knew my name? These neighbors were officially way too much. The last thing I wanted to do was shake her hand, but I also feared confrontation more than most tortures, so I reached out and took it, nodding in lieu of speaking.

Daphne was one of those people who held your hand too long after the shaking was over—which made me regret the action even more. She squeezed tight, even pulling my hand closer to her, probably wondering why I never came to see my grandmother.

Meanwhile, I was wondering if she would ever give my hand back. Compiling a list of nonconfrontational ways to retrieve it, I'd come up with three solid options when she let go. Relief washed away the heat that had been rising to my cheeks.

"It's always great to meet a fellow flower sister." She beamed.

My eyelids blinked questions in Morse code. *What? Sister?*

"Daphne." She pointed to her chest. "Rosie." The finger swung around toward me.

I pursed my lips. I mean, rosemary plants grew flowers. The problem was she'd said Rosie. No one called me Rosie. Rosie felt like a person I wasn't, would never be. A woman with a playful gleam in her eye and an adventurous spirit. I was Rosemary, unassuming, easy to overlook, and I liked it that way.

At least, I thought I did.

Hearing her call me Rosie started a tiny pit of longing in my stomach to be something more than the girl who'd been sick, the girl who'd survived so much only to fade into the background.

"If Rosemary's smart, she'll take her stems and run far, far away from all of us," Mr. Suspenders murmured.

I kept my focus on Daphne, knowing I would gawk if I let myself look back at him. The frank way he spoke was both terrifying and exhilarating to me.

Daphne seemed to be an expert at ignoring his comments, confirming my suspicion that they knew each other.

"Well," she said, fluffing her hair again. "I'll let you get situated, but I wanted to ask a tiny favor." At this she cringed a little as if what she was about to ask wasn't tiny. "It's just, I'm not sure what your plans are—if you'll keep it a tea shop or not or if you'll sell the house."

Daphne was rambling. I glanced over at Mr. Suspenders. He pinched the bridge of his nose.

"I wanted to ask what you were doing with her stock of Women's Liber-tea." Daphne's gaze moved to the containers along the wall behind the bar. "I'm going through menopause, is all, and the blend helps me. I ran out the other day, and I didn't want to intrude, but …" She held out a handful of bills.

My pursed lips parted. "Oh."

She shoved the money into my hands. "Can I buy the rest of her stock?"

I regarded the guy who was either staying here or tending to the plants. Either way, he had to know more about this than me. But when I glanced back, Mr. Suspenders kept his gaze averted. With this clear refusal of eye contact came an obvious avoidance of responsibility. I was on my own with this one.

"I'm not sure what I'm doing with the place yet," I said cautiously, realizing that anything I said was bound to go straight into the Pebble Cove gossip mill once Daphne returned home. "I'd be happy to sell you one or two, but I should keep the rest in stock … just in case."

Daphne raised an eyebrow in interest. "You must've talked to Gretta, then."

I inclined my head, hoping that was enough of an admittance. I had, in fact, talked with Grandma's realtor, Gretta, on the phone yesterday. Besides warning me about the neighbor who would probably be here watering plants when I showed up, she'd informed me that while there *was* an offer on the table, it was much lower than what she thought was fair for the business and the house.

"And?" Daphne watched me. "Will you take her advice?"

"Uh …" I shrugged. "I don't know."

"Well, you're here, aren't you? I suppose that's something." Daphne waved a hand at me.

The woman wasn't wrong. I could've done all the signing and legal stuff remotely. I told myself that I needed to come see the place once more, to see how it felt to be here again. Since I hadn't ever gotten closure with Grandma, this was my odd way of trying to get it. I'm not sure what I'd been expecting. I'd missed my chance. I should've had Gretta fax me the sales papers to sign and been done with it.

But just as I couldn't let Daphne take Grandma's entire stock of Women's Liber-tea, I also couldn't seem to let this place go without saying goodbye.

Sliding a few bills out from the large wad she'd offered

me a moment ago, Daphne said, "Okay, I'll take two bags, then."

I took the money and glanced back at the bar once more. Mr. Suspenders was watching us this time, but he still made no move to grab the bags for me or be helpful. I gave the room a scan, wondering if he'd even watered the plants or if he'd let that job go undone too.

Stifling a grumble, I made my way over to the bar and searched around. "Can you point out where she keeps them?" I asked the guy, ducking to get a better view of the dark shelves on the backside of the bar.

"The bin all the way to the right," Daphne said, popping her head over the top of the bar and almost making me gasp in surprise.

I hadn't asked her, but she must've known Mr. Suspenders wouldn't help me. My attention tracked over to the wicker baskets lined up under the bar and realized they bore small tags. She was right; the one to the far right had "Women's Liber-tea" written across it in my grandmother's delicate scrawl. Pulling two of the prepackaged bags out of the bin, I handed them over.

"Thank you, dear." Daphne hugged them to her chest. "I'll see you tomorrow." She waved over her shoulder as she turned to leave, clomping away in the same manner she'd arrived.

Tomorrow? I cringed.

I held a hand up in a wave, too tired to give in to my curiosity. Tomorrow, I'd be sure to lock the front door.

"Oh, I almost forgot," Daphne said, turning around.

My shoulders hunched in response, but I tried to combat the unsociable reaction with a friendly lift of my eyebrows.

"I'm very sorry about your loss." Daphne's face squished

into a kind smile. "Helen was a lovely woman, and we're all going to miss her, well—everyone but Carl." She chuckled.

"Thank you," I said with a nod. "Who's Carl?"

She jabbed a thumb to her right. "Your neighbor on the other side. You drove through his property to get here."

"Oh, right." *Another neighbor? Then where did Mr. Suspenders live?* This was becoming more confusing by the second. "Carl didn't like my grandma?"

"He doesn't like anyone, but no, especially not your grandma." Daphne clicked her tongue. "At least Helen's at peace now. I sure hope when it's my time, I can go in my sleep like she did."

She waved one last time and then disappeared down the hall. In keeping with his manner, Mr. Suspenders had a surly comment to add to Daphne's even though the front door already closed behind her.

"Oh, Daphne." He tsked. "You *don't* want to go like Helen. Not unless you'd like to be murdered too."

I gasped. The room spun.

Murdered?

By the time my vision cleared, and I turned around, Mr. Suspenders had disappeared.

2

I blinked at the now empty room.

The surprise of Mr. Suspenders' words, added to his sudden disappearance, caused confusion to swim about me in a dizzying daze.

Murdered? But my grandma died in her sleep. Hadn't she?

It was possible I'd heard him incorrectly.

Sure. That could be it.

As my foggy thoughts cleared, my shock gave way to anger. Normal people didn't say terrible things like that and leave. I didn't care how ill-disposed to small talk Mr. Surly Suspenders seemed; he had some explaining to do.

A wall of worry hit me face-first as I wondered if he could've been the one who had hurt her. I shook my head. No, surly as he was, he had an air about him that was … not kind exactly, but not threatening either. Plus Daphne hadn't seemed scared of him or of leaving me here alone with him.

Without overthinking the situation anymore—as I had the tendency to do—I went in search of him. Had he left?

No doors had closed after Daphne left, so he must still be in the house. I turned toward the kitchen to investigate.

When I entered the room, my phone began buzzing. I fished it from my pocket. *Mom*, I guessed. The name flashing across the screen confirmed my suspicions.

Instead of answering it, I did something very unlike myself—I hesitated. Usually, I wouldn't think twice about taking a call from Mom. She was my best friend, my only remaining family, and the person I trusted the most.

But that word: *murdered*, kept cycling through my brain as my thumb hovered over the answer button.

Mom knew me too well. She would be able sense something was wrong. I needed to wait until I talked to Mr. Suspenders. I pressed the ignore button and cringed as I shoved the phone back in my pocket, waiting for the inevitable voice mail.

In the meantime, I started my search in the kitchen. It was empty. The glass bird still hung in the window. Memories of the morning sunlight reflecting off the colored glass as Grandma and I made pancakes for breakfast came flooding back to me. I would sit on the counter helping her measure ingredients and stir. She would pop blueberries, raspberries, or pieces of banana in my mouth like I was a little baby bird. I didn't know how I felt about those memories, so I focused on my task to locate Mr. Suspenders.

From the kitchen, I climbed the narrow staircase up to the second floor, where my grandmother's bedroom and her guest room were located. The rooms were dark and quiet. I peered into her small bedroom. A large antique clock ticked away from atop an oak dresser. A light summer quilt had been neatly spread over the bed and tucked under each corner.

Who'd made her bed? I wondered. Had it been Mr.

Suspenders or someone else? I didn't know if my grandma had friends. Maybe she didn't have any, which would explain why some random guy my age was taking care of her plants. My grandpa had died when I was very young, so she'd been alone for a long time. But even so, it seemed odd for her to have left me her home, especially after our estrangement. Was that because she had no one else to leave it to or because she still felt a connection to me after all this time?

The questions piled up, but I had no answers. I turned around to check the guest bedroom. Nothing but memories in there either. The dull ache returned in my chest as I scanned the room Mom and Dad used to share. I remembered climbing into bed with them in the mornings, sandwiching myself between them, covered in blankets and love and laughter. Sometimes Grandma would find us and joke like she would climb in too, and we would all giggle until we were awake and ready for a day of beachcombing.

And while the memories made me smile and served as a reminder of all the great times I'd experienced here, they were from a different time. That had been before everything changed, before the accident, before my diagnosis, before the fight. Old wooden floors creaked under me as I turned to check the bathroom situated in the middle of the two rooms and found that empty as well.

"Hello?" I called out, pausing on the landing at the top of the stairs. "Sir? Mr. Suspenders?" The volume of my questions ebbed with my doubt. My words echoed off the white and black tiles of the bathroom floor and shower behind me. No response.

Speaking of responses, I checked my phone. No voice mail from Mom—yet. Yeesh, it must be a long one. I gripped the phone in my hand as I continued my search.

While clomping down the front stairway, I paused at the small window on the landing. Through it I spied the neighbor's house, bits of the stained wood and stark white moldings peeked through the line of treelike rhododendrons outside.

Carl's house, I mused, remembering Daphne's comment about how he hated my grandmother. *Did he have something to do with her death?* I wondered. Was his hatred for her why Mr. Suspenders thought she'd been killed instead of dying in her sleep?

Frustration leaked out of me in a huff. I couldn't answer any of these questions if I couldn't find the man who'd triggered them.

The rest of the stairway passed by in a blur. Taking a hard left, I walked through the study and adjoining library where I used to sleep on a cot when we stayed here. The floor-to-ceiling windows created the illusion of being outside, right in the middle of her wildflower garden. I remembered gazing up at the stars and watching the moon as I fell asleep each night, lulled into slumber by the crashing waves just outside the ancient panes of glass.

I checked the downstairs restroom, now designated for tea shop customers. Nothing. I chewed on my lip as I returned to the main tearoom space.

The house was empty.

Where'd he go?

I put my hands on my hips, stepping closer to the bar. Had he been hiding behind it this whole time? I leaned forward to get a better view, but it was as empty as the rest of the house.

My fingers swept across the lacquered wood. It held stacks of menus and small mason jars, each filled with a tea light. Behind the bar, there was a wall of shelves, stacked with jar after jar of dried leaves, labeled with a careful, curving script, handwritten to label each blend.

It was the tea lover's equivalent to a wall full of books in the eyes of a bibliophile like me.

The large room was mostly windows on one side. Lofty picture windows spanned the space between the wood floor and the vaulted ceilings. The white-capped waves and pebbled beach visible through the windows took my breath away, much like the coastal wind sometimes did when a gust would hit me full force.

My phone buzzed in my hand, startling me from my reverie. *And that will be Mom's voicemail*, I thought. But it wasn't. Three rapid-fire texts came through instead.

Hey, sweetie ...

How's the house? Is it weird being back there?

Do you need me to come out?

Uh oh. Three questions in a row. Mom was officially having a hard time with me being here.

Pulling in a deep breath, I reminded myself that she only got intense like this because she loved me and worried about me. And honestly, the woman had reason to worry. When most parents' biggest worries were puberty and attitude, my mom was raising me alone, helping me fight a life-threatening disease. And she'd been by my side, my rock, through all of it.

As my thoughts drifted, my gaze strayed back to the view outside.

Just then, I spotted a man's silhouette out on the beach.

Mr. Suspenders.

Gotcha!

I typed up a quick message, telling Mom I couldn't talk, but that I loved her and would call later. Sliding my phone back in my pocket, I headed out the back door, onto the porch.

The salty sea air plastered my dark hair to my face. Sparrows' sharp chirps cut through the lengthy trills of songbirds. Tall, sage-and-lavender-colored grass grew all around the cottage, creeping right up to the edges of my grandmother's garden, which created a barrier from the wild coastline.

I stormed past it all, straight toward Mr. Suspenders.

He stood with his back to me, facing the water. I'd always found the waves mesmerizing to watch, and it seemed he did too by the way he stared out at the rolling water.

My feet slipped on the mixture of pebbles and sand as I approached him. The coastal wind swirled around me. Clouds rolled along above us, their movement making me even more unsteady. The crunch of my shoes on the rocky shore betrayed my approach.

But he didn't turn around.

"Hey," I called. My words broke and fell to pieces, dragged away by the wind.

Still nothing. He stood just as still, gazing out at the water.

As I stepped up to him, any confidence I'd gathered dispersed as quickly as tea leaves in the wind. Who was I kidding? I wasn't a *confront people* person. I was barely an *introduce myself* person. But the word "murdered" simmered inside my brain, pushing me out of my comfort zone.

I needed to know.

"I—have a question," I said, stepping closer.

The man didn't move. At that point, I was right behind him, his broad shoulders looming in front of me.

Murdered. The word swept over me, around me, behind me. It pushed me forward like a gust of wind.

"Sir," I said more forcefully, then I reached forward to tap him in the shoulder.

But my hand went right through him.

3

A chill washed over my fingers as if I'd wafted them through a cloud of liquid nitrogen. My whole body froze stiff, making the dry-ice comparison even more real. Even when he turned around, I remained unable to move a limb.

He jumped in surprise, his wide eyes flicked down to my hand, now sticking through his chest.

Our eyes met. The ocean wind whipped around me, and the waves moving in the background made my vision unsteady.

As of its own accord, my hand moved to the left, wafting through his collarbone. The chill intensified. My fingers curled, though I couldn't see them through his opaque body.

As if I'd ever encountered a body that wasn't opaque, I scoffed inwardly, pulling my hand back to myself.

"You can see me?" he asked, breaking my thought process. All his cocky confidence from earlier was gone. In fact, his tone shook.

When I met his eyes again, he was watching me with that intense gaze, leaving goose bumps in its wake. I couldn't even begin to answer his question. What was I even seeing? Things like this only happened in the books I shelved in my job at the library.

Daphne's lack of reaction to him earlier now made sense. What if she hadn't been ignoring his comments? What if she hadn't even heard them? He wasn't the neighbor here to take care of the plants.

The scariness of the situation wrapped around me as my thoughts careened toward what this might mean. My heart raced, and my breath became shallow. *It's impossible,* I thought, shaking my head. I didn't believe in ghosts. That sounded too much like a conspiracy my tea-leaf-reading grandma would've bought into. But not me. I was rational, like my mother.

I backed away from him.

As I was about to turn and run, his face softened, and he held up his hands.

"Please. Wait."

Only two words left his lips, but the emotion wrapped around them was so intense that it held me in place. Memories of myself making a similar plea crowded in my mind—the kids at school skirting around me, scooting farther from me at lunch, even running away from me at recess.

Please.

Even after the teacher explained to them that leukemia wasn't contagious, that they couldn't get sick by being my friend.

Wait.

I stopped.

He took a slow step forward. "I've—It's been so long since I've met someone who can see me … you caught me off guard. I didn't mean to frighten you."

I focused on breathing.

He stood up straighter. "I'm Asher."

My brain struggled to compute. He had a name. Asher. He looked real.

"What are you?" I finally croaked.

I surveyed his body, focusing on his tweed pants and the suspenders I'd used as his moniker. He wore a white linen button-up shirt underneath the suspenders, tucked into his pants. Was what I'd mistaken as hipster attire actually old-timey clothing?

"What are you doing here?" I asked, pointing behind me. "In my grandmother's house?"

"It was my house, back when I was alive." Asher's countenance had completely shifted. The surly and sarcastic man from before was gone. Now his blue eyes held an earnestness, an undeniable need.

Back when I was alive … Confirming he wasn't anymore.

The sound of the waves normally had a calming white-noise effect, but at his statement, the crashing became overwhelming.

"I'm sorry," I said. "I can't …" I didn't know how to finish that sentence.

"I died about a hundred years ago." He caught my gaze with his.

I coughed, not sure why hearing him say it aloud made such a difference. "You're truly a ghost?"

He tipped his head to one side. "I've always preferred *spirit*, but sure."

My throat went hot, and a metallic flavor coated my tongue. I swallowed. "But you don't look like a ghost." I rolled my eyes at myself. "Not that I expect you to be wearing a sheet with two eyeholes. It's just—you look *solid*, is all."

If I hadn't seen my hand pass through him, as it

would've through a cloud, I wouldn't have believed it myself. He appeared to be the same as any person I'd ever seen.

"I'm at my strongest here, where I spent most of my life. Maybe that's why you can see me so clearly." Asher wet his lips and glanced down at the ground.

"Why did you say my grandma was murdered?"

His face darkened, and he turned toward me. "Because she told me."

A gasp escaped my mouth. "Is she a ghost too? Am I going to see her?" Simultaneous feelings of excitement and worry flooded my heart.

Shrugging, he said, "She's here in a sense, though not like I am. When a spirit is in turmoil, they tend not to settle for a while. I didn't regain sentience for almost two years after my death, so it may be awhile until she can take a form you might see."

Turmoil.

That word kicked me in the gut. I sank down onto the sand, ducking against an intense gust of sea wind. When it passed by, I peeked up from under my hair. Asher knelt beside me. He wore concern as plainly as he wore those suspenders.

"Everyone thinks she died in her sleep." I pinched my lips together. "It was her heart."

He settled onto his butt, though it made no indent in the rocks and sand like mine. "She *was* having issues with her heart, but that's not what killed her. I watched her take her nightly medications. She became short of breath, and her pupils were dilated, and then she went to bed. Moments later, her spirit floated past me. She looked straight at me for the first time and said, 'I've been poisoned. Tell Rosemary I'm sorry.' Then she disappeared."

My body swayed. This wasn't happening. I sucked in a quick breath. "Did you see who did it?"

At my question, Asher's jaw clenched tight. His broad shoulders fell. "No. I had just come inside when she was getting ready for bed. I like to watch the sun set." He pointed to my left toward the lighthouse that sat at the tip of the spit that created Pebble Cove.

Asher's words blurred together, creating a buzzing sensation in my ears.

"How are you the only one who knows this? Didn't the doctor figure out the cause of death?"

He clasped his hands behind his back. "When they were here, the medical team said she'd been diagnosed with heart disease, and there was no need to do an autopsy."

Shutting my eyes tight, I pulled in a long breath. *This can't be happening. This can't be happening.* I wasn't sure if I was talking about the ghost sitting in front of me or his insistence that my grandmother was murdered. Or both.

Suddenly it all became too much. The wind beat against my chest and I couldn't breathe. I scrambled to my feet. Swiping my hair out of my face, I looked at Asher.

"I—uh—need time, and space . . . and maybe food. I'm —" But before I finished my sentence, a shape in the water caught my eye.

As the waves pulled back, they revealed a form laying in the wet sand below the tide line. At first I thought it was a piece of driftwood, the gnarled base of an oak. The waves raced forward again, crashing over and covering the shape. But when they retreated the next time, I knew I wasn't looking at driftwood.

"What's wrong?" Asher asked, his face contorting into a frown.

I gawked at the water for a moment more before returning my attention to him.

"It's …" I couldn't find the words, so I pointed toward the crashing waves. "Is that …?" A shiver wound up the skin of my back like a rolling pinprick as I spit out the broken question.

I could tell the exact moment Asher caught sight of what I'd seen because his Adam's apple dipped as he swallowed.

My feet started forward as if of their own accord. They slipped and stumbled through the sand and pebbles, mirroring my total mental disequilibrium. After a few sliding steps, I made it to the firmer wet sand and stopped, reveling in the minuscule amount of stability it provided.

Another shiver ran over my body as Asher came up next to me soundlessly. He didn't stop but approached the shape. His feet made no imprints in the sand nor did they disturb the water as he walked into the waves.

But if his ghostly form was chilling, it turned out to be nothing compared to what he said when he looked up a moment later.

"Call the police. This man is dead."

4

There were many signs the man was dead. First, he wasn't moving. Second, he appeared to have washed up onshore from farther out in the ocean based on the condition of his clothing. Third, and most telling, the body was bloated and … not entirely intact. His skin had a grayish color to it.

But in my shock, I didn't immediately follow Asher's request. Instead, I came closer to him and the thing we now recognized as a man's body. I stopped at the edge of the water.

"Can you sense his spirit too?" I asked as I approached a confused Asher—who had to be wondering why the heck I wasn't calling the police.

Asher narrowed his eyes at me. "No, it looks like he's been dead for a while."

Closer examination of the body proved Asher told the truth. I spun around, dry heaving for a moment before setting my hands on my knees and catching my breath.

It was from this position that I eventually called the police.

"There's a body in the water, near Tea by the Sea on Pebble Beach off Misty Drive," I informed the dispatcher in rushed tones as if timing mattered at all.

Information I did NOT tell the operator: There's a ghost standing next to me.

"I have a unit coming out to you now. Is the person deceased?" she asked as if we could just as well have been talking about the weather.

I gulped. "Yes." I hoped she wouldn't ask me to explain how I knew this, really not wanting to describe what lay in the sand before me.

Proving that I sounded as unsteady as I felt, she said, "I'll send Dr. Ellis too. She also works as our medical examiner." The quick clicking of fingers across a keyboard sounded in the background. She asked for my name and address just in case. I gave both to her. "Rosemary, I'll stay on the line with you until they get there so you're not alone."

Almost blurting out that I wasn't alone, I pressed my lips together tight. That was close. Even though Asher stood nearby—appearing as real as the beach surrounding me—as far as anyone else was concerned, I was alone.

"Thank you," I whispered into the phone.

When the police arrived, I would need to be careful.

Looking up at Asher, I caught him observing me. His blue eyes flicked away the moment mine met with his. I kept the phone pressed to my ear as Asher moved closer, standing next to me so his shoulder almost touched mine—though I knew from experience that even if it did, I wouldn't feel it.

I wanted to talk with him, to ask him more questions, all the questions. Instead, we stood side by side, watching the waves in silence. Well, *we* were silent. The ocean churned and crashed in front of us, creating an engulfing din that wrapped around me. Shivering, I pulled my hood on and tucked my long hair inside, happy for the reprieve from the wind.

The skin on the back of my neck prickled, and I turned to see a white-haired man standing in the window of the house next door. Carl. His scowl was clear, even from this distance, and I turned away, wondering if he could see the body next to me.

The tide moved out, so more of the body was visible after each wave. The man appeared to have been middle aged. He was balding and a little overweight. A visual check of his right finger showed there wasn't a wedding ring. His clothes were business casual, a pair of khakis and a cotton button up. The button up was a light blue color the likes of which I'd seen on countless businessmen who made their way into the library each day.

The one unusual attribute of the shirt, however, were the vibrant blue buttons running up the front of the shirt and closing the cuffs around the man's wrists. I'd seen white, clear, even pearlescent buttons before adorning such a shirt, but never the vibrant blue color of these. The other odd thing about the buttons was the absence of quite a few of them. Being of a rotund form, I wondered if the man's large belly had strained the thread so much that the buttons had burst off, especially in his bloated state. Or had the sea ripped the buttons off?

A door slammed somewhere behind me, the sound of it carried on the wind. I turned to see a small group making their way toward us, picking through the sparse, sage-colored grass and ring of driftwood that acted as a barrier between Grandma's garden and the beach.

They looked as if their goal was to dress as differently from each other as possible. The younger of the two men wore a blue EMT uniform. His blond hair blew into his face as the coastal winds hit him full force. He appeared to be about my age. The older man wore a police officer's uniform. Gray along his temples and sideburns whispered stories of experience that the grim lines on his leathery face only confirmed. The third in the party was a woman. Her smart wrap dress was confusingly paired with bright green rain boots.

In case she has to step in the water, I realized. Which meant she was probably the Dr. Ellis the dispatcher had mentioned.

Reminded of the person on the other end of the line, I croaked out, "They're here." The words left my mouth at the same time a large gust of air whooshed into the microphone, and I hoped she'd heard me.

"Okay, I'll let you go, then." The call ended with a click before I could answer.

I deposited the phone into my pocket and trained my eyes on Asher.

"Do you want me to stay near?" he asked.

"I would like that," I said with a small smile, noticing that though his dark hair was about as long as the blond man approaching, it didn't move in the wind at all.

I could've sworn I saw a hint of a happiness twitch at the corner of Asher's mouth at my request that he stay. But I couldn't focus on whether or not the ghost was smiling because the approaching trio reached me. I turned to face them, my fingers grasping at the drawstrings of my hood as the wind threatened to snatch it off.

The EMT gave me a grim nod before bypassing me. The doctor did the same, though her lips pulled into an apologetic grimace before she stepped up to the body. The older man, however, stopped right in front of me.

After glancing around me at the body for a moment, he

asked, "You're the Rosemary Woodmere who called this in?"

I confirmed I was.

"I'm the chief of police, Raymond Clemenson. Can you tell me about how you came upon the scene?" He pulled out a flip-style notepad and clicked open a pen.

The chief exuded a gruff, authoritative air, but I caught something gentle behind his stoic exterior. It was this kind of softness amid firmness that made Atticus Finch such a captivating character to me. Then it hit me. Just as Atticus Finch had, this chief reminded me of my father. My need for his approval skyrocketed.

He cleared his throat, reminding me I still had yet to answer his question about how I'd found the body.

"Sorry, um … we were out here walking when I noticed something in the water. At first I thought it was driftwood, but then I got a closer look and saw that it was a man—or it used to be." I rubbed my hands up and down my arms.

"We?" the chief asked, brown eyes piercing as he held my gaze. "There was someone else here with you?" He scanned the beach.

My cheeks burned despite the cool wind on my face. *Had I said we?* I cursed myself for my weird fatherly thoughts about the police chief. They must've flustered me enough to make me forget my warning to myself.

I laughed, cringing over at Asher before turning back to the chief.

"Oh, haha. No, just me and my thoughts. Sorry."

Heat spread from my chest up into my neck as the chief inspected me.

Finally, he scratched a few words onto the notepad he held, face unreadably grim. Observing the way his features set into a frown, I saw how he'd earned his wrinkles. The few times Chief Clemenson's eyes flicked back up to me as he wrote cemented my worry that he hadn't quite bought my explanation.

Asher moved behind the man and read over his shoulder. He craned his neck and squinted, the corners of his mouth tipped downward.

"He thinks you're lying," Asher said.

I was about to scold him for speaking, when I remembered I was the only one who could hear him.

Moving to the left, Asher continued, "He's adding you to his suspect list."

"What?" I blurted out, before slapping my hand over my mouth.

The chief glanced up, the lines in his forehead deepening.

"Uh—*what* is that?" I pointed out at the water.

He spun around, peering in the direction I'd indicated, before turning back toward me. "I'm not seeing anything."

I squinted at the waves. "Oh, I thought I saw something. I guess it's gone. Maybe it was a whale." Heat washed over my face.

He looked again, but I could tell it was only to humor me. When Chief Clemenson turned back, his eyes combed up and down me for a moment as if I might be hiding my crazy in my shoes.

"You can go wait up at your house. I'll have more questions for you." He turned toward the doctor and the EMT.

I nodded in shock as he walked away. "Chief?" I said, stopping him.

He raised an eyebrow as he pivoted.

"My grandma, she passed away a couple weeks ago. What if I told you there are a few things that are suspicious about her death?" I kept my gaze on the chief, but I could feel Asher watching me.

"Helen?" the chief of police asked. "Helen had a heart condition. The only suspicious thing about her death is why none of her family showed until now." With that, he walked away.

My shoulders sank under the weight of his words. Feet sliding in the sand as I walked, I made my way back to Grandma's garden.

"Hey, are you okay?" Asher asked.

I jumped, not realizing he'd followed me. "Just great."

The phrase was short, fueled by frustration. Asher's face tightened as I snapped at him.

"I'm sorry." I let my gaze fall to my feet. "I don't mean to be snippy. It's … what he said back there …"

I wasn't about to admit to this ghost I'd just met how much I wanted the chief's approval because he'd reminded me of my father. I definitely didn't want to admit to the extent it hurt that he didn't believe me, that he suspected me.

Asher furrowed his brow as if he knew, anyway. "Yeah, sorry. That was harsh. Here, come inside. I think there might be a few things to eat in the cupboard."

Warmth wrapped around me as we entered the beach house. Not only because we were out of the wind, but because of Asher's kindness. And now that he mentioned it, I became aware of how hungry I was. I'd had an early breakfast before hitting the road and hadn't had anything to eat since.

Asher walked straight into the kitchen. I followed behind. He pointed to a cabinet. "There might be some cookies in a tin in here. If you want tea, she keeps a personal stash in this one." He gestured to the next cabinet over.

"From the pallor of your skin, I think a cup of tea would do you good."

My body felt numb, and the initial warmth I'd experienced stepping inside was wearing off. I nodded at his suggestions and got to work. Setting the kettle on the stove, I turned on the burner. Then I plucked a mug off the shelf and set it on the counter. I'd never been one to drink tea, so the loose-leaf options I found in jars when I opened the cabinet left me furrowing my forehead in confusion.

"There's a measuring spoon in there with the jars. Scoop two spoonfuls into the little wire basket over there. There should also be a digital timer in there. Four minutes to steep, and you should be set," Asher said as if reading my mind again. "And I think you should try the one labeled Home."

Not in a space to make my own decisions, I followed his directions. As the digital display counted down the minutes, I turned to face him. A grin spread across his face.

"Sorry," he said, wiping a hand along his jawline as if the motion might erase the smile. "I know what just happened isn't a happy thing. It's been a long time since I had someone to talk to."

I tried to return the smile, but a burning question took precedence. "What are we going to do about that?" I gestured toward the beach, goose bumps prickling up my arms as I remembered the body lying in the waves. "How are you not more freaked out? Does this kind of thing happen a lot?"

Asher grimaced. "Unfortunately, yes. You know about Desperation Cliff five miles north?"

I nodded, remembering Grandma and I walking up that way one day. Large, rocky cliffs ran the length of most of the surrounding coastline, but there was a mile-long stretch that was treacherous. Between the height, the sheer face, and the inhospitable craggy beach below, the cliffs had earned their name.

"My grandma wouldn't ever let me go there. She said many people had died from waves that crashed them into the rocks."

"That's not the only thing." Asher's tone was somber. "That cliff is a common place for people to jump."

"Commit suicide?"

"Yeah, we get a few each year." Asher's shoulders slumped. "Him washing up on your beach is probably just a terrible coincidence."

My focus drifted to the fridge, to the half-dozen sticky notes stuck to the surface. They were notes Grandma had left herself, ranging from reminders of what to pick up at the grocery store, to people to talk to about different subjects, and even one that simply said, "Frogs?" As odd as it felt to be learning about my grandma like this, posthumously, there was an element of comfort to being surrounded by signs of her life.

While I mused, silence sat between me and Asher, making the moment when the timer beeped to life even more jarring. Asher's eyes lit up, and I jolted out of my stupor. Turning off the timer, I poured some of the now caramel-colored liquid into a mug and paused. I opened my mouth to ask if he wanted some and then stopped myself.

Right.

Instead, I grasped the mug with both hands as if it were some kind of lifeline, some way to forget the terrible things I'd seen and learned today. The steam swirling off it smelled of cinnamon, cardamom, and vanilla. My eyes closed as I breathed it in.

"Oh, wow." My eyes flashed open. "That's amazing."

I brought the mug to my lips and sipped. The warm liquid filled my mouth, settling in a cozy ball in my stomach.

Asher pointed again to the first cabinet, and I opened it, locating a tin can of shortbread cookies.

"They might be expired, but at least they're edible." He grinned and gestured to my mug. "I knew you would love that blend."

I took another sip as I fished a cookie from the tin. "How? We just met."

"It was your grandmother's favorite. She used to tell people how alike you two were."

Tears pricked at my eyes. "She talked about me?" I asked, taking a gulp of the hot tea after that, hoping to hold the worst of the tears at bay.

Asher's head bobbed. "All the time. She never talked about why you didn't come around anymore—the rest of the town speculated about it when she would leave the room—but it was as if she couldn't help but talk about you."

Suddenly all the emotions surrounding the day piled onto me. I'd spent so much of my life trying to distance myself from my grandma. But now, back in her house, nothing seemed severe enough to justify not talking to her for so long.

Heck, she'd been right about ghosts; maybe she'd been right about everything else.

5

Just as I was wolfing down my fourth stale cookie, a knock sounded on the glass of the back door. I jumped and coughed as crumbs went down my windpipe.

Asher arched a single eyebrow but followed me when I got up and padded into the next room. Chief Clemenson stood on the porch wearing a stoic expression as cut and clean as his uniform.

I blinked against a gust of wind as I opened the door.

"May I come in?" he asked, squinting against the flurry.

I stepped aside and let him enter, determined to make this interaction better than our last. "Did you find out anything about the man?"

The chief cocked his head. "Quite a bit." He paused in a way that made me unsure whether or not he had more to say.

I waited for a beat before asking, "Good?"

The police chief's jaw jutted forward. "Miss Woodmere, you said you didn't recognize him. Is that right?"

I scoffed, "Not to be indelicate, sir, but there wasn't much there to go by."

"Anything about his clothes? Nothing looked familiar?" the chief asked.

Other than his bright blue buttons, nothing had looked even remotely interesting and definitely not familiar. "No, not at all," I said. After a moment, I narrowed my eyes. "Why?"

The chief took a seat at the nearest table in the tea shop. I sat across from him. He took out his phone and pulled up a picture. Turning it toward me, he set the phone on the table. The picture showed a man in his forties with dark, thinning hair and a toothy, white smile.

"This was him. His name was Frank Mastronardi. When my officers contacted his office, his secretary told us he was here to stay at The Pines Restorative Center for the week, but he never checked in."

I stared at him, unsure what that was or why he would tell me this.

"Do you want to tell me why when my officers located his vehicle at the top of Desperation Cliff, they found only one name in his appointment book? Yours."

"Mine?" I gasped out the question.

"He had your name and the address to this house." The chief folded his arms on top of the table and leaned closer to me. "And then he just washes up on the beach in front of your house. That's quite the coincidence, don't you think?"

Gulping, I nodded.

"You do?" He raised a silver speckled eyebrow.

"No, you don't," Asher said, rushing to my side. "He's trying to get you to implicate yourself; don't fall into his trap."

I crossed my arms. "Uh, I mean, it's odd, but I swear I don't know that man. I've never seen him in my life, and I've never heard that name. I think I would remember a last name like that."

The chief sat back, and I glanced over at Asher in thanks.

"Okay, if you want to play it that way. Don't leave town, Miss Woodmere." He got up.

Play it what way? I wondered.

"But I was only supposed to be here for a few days, tops. I have to sign some papers and then I'm leaving." I shoved my chair back as I stood too.

The chief pushed his hands into his pockets. "We'll try to figure out what happened as soon as possible. I'm sorry if that's not what you were hoping for, but I think the late Mr. Mastronardi is even more inconvenienced than you." He turned and let himself out the back door.

"As if this day could get any weirder …" I said aloud as he cut through the garden pathway out toward the front of the house.

Asher's lips pressed into a grim line. "He had your name on him?"

"And they found his car up at the cliff. All of that sounds like he committed suicide, right?" I paused "So why does he think I had something to do with any of it?"

Running his hand across his chin, Asher paced in front of me. "Don't worry. You're innocent, right?" He regarded me as if he wasn't sure what my answer would be.

"Of course I am!" I threw my hands up.

Asher backed away. "Okay, sorry. Making sure. I just met you."

I scoffed, "The ghost I just met is making sure I'm not a murderer." I let out a dry laugh.

My sentence, meant as a lighthearted joke, instead highlighted the craziness of my day. Was this my reality now? I was talking to a ghost about being a suspect in an actual murder. The chief's words pressed in on me, trapping me like the squirrel that got caught in our library drop bin last year.

My chest heaved up and down in rapid breaths, I started pacing.

"I can't do this. I can't stay here. First, you tell me my grandma, who I haven't spoken to in fifteen years, has been murdered, then you're a ghost, a dead body washes up on the beach, and I'm somehow a suspect in it all." Reciting the list of problems made my head spin.

Worry clawed at my throat in hot waves. My wild eyes scanned the house, searching for a way out. My keys lit up like a beacon. I grabbed them off the table, grasping them in my hand so tight I knew they would leave a mark.

"I was only supposed to stay for a few days, and now I'm not supposed to leave? I *need* to leave. I have to get out of here. None of this is happening." I laughed. "It's all in my imagination." My eyes widened. "That's it. I'm hallucinating because I'm hungry, and all I've eaten in hours are stale cookies. I'm going to eat real food, and all of this will go away."

Asher studied me like a bomb that might go off at any second.

I waved a hand at him. "I don't know why I'm telling you any of this, since you aren't real."

In my manic state, I heard him say, "Rosemary … just take one breath."

I froze, ice water surged through my veins. "What?"

"Start with one deep breath and then another." He watched me carefully.

Tears pooled in the corners of my eyes. "She used to say that."

His lips pulled into a sad smile. "I know."

The reality of this unreal situation came crashing back down on me. I could deny it, insist I was going crazy, pretend it wasn't happening all I wanted. It wouldn't change the facts. This was something I couldn't run from, couldn't hide from until it went away.

I sighed. "Can't we wait until her spirit settles to ask her who did this?" I asked.

Asher tensed. "I don't remember how I died. None of the other spirits I've encountered do either. I think it's why ghosts seek the help of humans so often. They're trying to piece it together. I doubt your grandma would remember anything from the night she died."

My heart ached for both of them. I couldn't tell if it was worse not to know what happened or to relive the possibly awful last moments of one's life repeatedly.

"Her spirit won't be able to move on if her killer isn't brought to justice?"

Asher shrugged. "It's all about unfinished business. That could be the reason she can't move on." He cleared his throat. "Or it could be something else."

That he had yet to move on made me wonder what was keeping him here, but by the way he wasn't meeting my eyes, he either didn't know or wasn't ready to share that information yet.

"Well, I'd say it's obvious the police won't be any help," I said. My disappointment about Chief Clemenson's distrust in me sat at the bottom of my stomach like a rock. "So if I have to stick around for a while anyway, we might as well find out who did this to her."

Asher took a step forward. "I know this is a lot to take in, but running away from it won't help. I can talk you through it."

I took one breath. Then another. Settling into a chair, I took a third.

"This is real?"

He nodded.

"And I have to stay and deal with it?"

"I'm afraid so."

"Okay, I think I'm going to need a minute." I pulled out my phone.

He squinted. "What are you doing?"

"A minute and a pizza, actually. That's what I need."

When a knock sounded at the front door six minutes later, I let my eyebrows rise, impressed. Even in the bustling city of Portland where a pizza place was around a corner from me, it took them at least twenty minutes to cook and deliver my pies.

I was all set to give the delivery person the best tip in the history of pizza deliveries for this faster-than-the-speed-of-light arrival. But when I opened the door, the man standing on the other side was definitely not here to deliver a pizza.

He had about ten inches on me and a good ten years. His dark gray suit warned of self-satisfied tendencies, something his slicked-back blond hair and bright white teeth further confirmed. His sharp, spicy cologne forced its way inside, making my nose tingle and itch.

"That's the mayor," Asher said, almost making me jump. I hadn't even noticed he'd followed me to the door.

Focusing my attention on the live man in front of me instead of the dead one behind me, I said, "Hello."

The man shoved a large hand in my direction. "Hi,

there. Name's Sam Hoff, I'm the mayor here in Pebble Cove."

Asher let out a quiet, "See?" from over my shoulder.

I shook his hand. "Hi, Mayor." My words came out slow and wary, sounding much less like a greeting and more like an accusation. I peered around him, still holding out a little hope he might have my pizza with him.

"May I come in?" he asked with a sweeping gesture toward the tearoom.

I stepped back, and he strutted inside. Asher followed him, his posture stiffening. Inside the tearoom, Mayor Hoff glanced around before turning his gaze back to me.

"I wanted to make sure you were settling in okay. Do you have questions about our town?" He flashed another bright white smirk in my direction.

Asher scoffed, "Sure, *that's* why you came."

"Do you greet every new person face-to-face?" I asked, ignoring Asher's commentary.

The mayor inclined his head. "Why not? Small towns, am I right?" He chuckled. "In all seriousness, I hear you had a bit of a surprise today."

Which one? I thought to myself with a snort. Deciding there was no way he could know about Grandma's murder or the ghost standing next to him, I figured he was talking about the dead body on the beach.

I stayed silent. Over the years, I'd learned that I needed to talk much less than one would think. So if I was feeling awkward or overwhelmed, my default was to stay quiet. People would fill in the space with their own words.

"Tragic." The mayor swiped at his upper lip, which I noticed was beaded with sweat. "You know the man?"

Shaking my head vehemently, I caught a spark of intensity just behind the mayor's eyes. He was fishing for information. Ah, so that's why he was here. Understanding washed over me. He'd probably been sent over by Police Chief Clemenson to do more digging.

"I heard he knew you," Mayor Hoff said as if proving my point. "And he came from Portland, like you." The man raised a blond eyebrow.

"Portland is a big city. It's not like Pebble Cove. We don't know everyone who lives there like you guys do down here." Feeling a little fiery, I added, "The mayor of Portland also doesn't make house calls."

A wide grin spread across his handsome face. "Of course." He laughed, but there was something about the motivation behind it that made it seem more like a threat than a happy gesture. "So you really haven't ever heard of Frank Mastronardi? You didn't meet with him or even speak to him?" I felt like if the mayor had a small desk lamp, he would've turned the shade up to point it at me like in an interrogation room.

I shook my head again.

The mayor's eyes searched my face in a way that made me want to shiver. Then his gaze settled on the pile of political signs I'd noticed earlier, leaning up against the staircase to the second floor.

The mayor's jaw clenched, causing a muscle to flex in his cheek. "Well, nice to meet you, Rosealee. I'll see myself out."

"It's Rosemary, you cad," Asher called after him as the man's large form retreated from the room.

I smiled over at Asher in thanks, but the whole encounter had me reeling. If these people believed I had something to do with that man's death, I was in way more trouble than I thought.

6

Once the mayor left, I paced and breathed during the seventeen and a half minutes it took my pizza to arrive. The confusing visit/interrogation made my hunger even more pronounced. I almost hugged the poor teenager who delivered the food.

"Okay. Where do we go from here?" I asked once I'd finished my first slice.

Asher scratched at his temple. "Next door, of course."

I spun toward him, flicking a little sauce in his direction. "Because you think this angry Carl neighbor had something to do with all of this like I do?"

"Wrong direction." Asher pointed the other way.

"Daphne?" My mouth fell open. "I mean, I wouldn't have suspected her, but I guess people aren't always what they seem."

Asher chuckled. "She didn't have anything to do with your grandma's death." He paused, studying the ceiling before adding, "At least, I hope she didn't. The woman knows everything that happens in Pebble Cove. If someone had it in for your grandma, she would know."

"So we just walk over there?" I asked.

"*You* just walk over there," he said, shooting me a pointed look.

I touched my nose then took another bite of pizza. "Thanks for the reminder. Yes, I'm going to walk over there and …"

"Apologize for not being chattier earlier," Asher suggested. He rolled his shoulders back. I wondered if it was a habit left over from living or if he could still feel the stretch.

"*I* wasn't chatty enough?" I asked, my voice wavering in my disbelief. "Psh. You're one to talk. Do you want to know what my nickname for you was until we started talking?"

His eyes sparkled. "Definitely."

"Mr. Surly Suspenders."

Asher let out a booming laugh and hooked his thumbs through his suspenders. "I like it. Well then, I apologize for my behavior before. When no one can hear you, you stop worrying about how the things you say sound."

I smiled. "I don't ever stop worrying about what I say. Mostly, I opt to not say anything to people."

"Huh, you seem pretty chatty to me."

He was right. I'd been talking with him, no problem. Maybe the fact that he wasn't alive gave me a weird freedom to be myself, not to worry what he thought. Maybe I could be a Rosie after all.

I brought the rest of my slice with me as I got ready to leave. I also grabbed an extra bag of the Women's Liber-tea blend, saying, "Just in case" when Asher gave me a questioning frown. Together, we walked outside and headed next door, toward Daphne Bertraud's yellow home.

Shooting me a sidelong glance as we walked, Asher asked, "What does pizza taste like?"

After swallowing my last bite, I said, "Omigosh, you've never tried pizza?" His face morphed into an exasperated expression that told me to think about it. I slapped my hand onto my forehead. "Of course you wouldn't. Well, it's doughy—like the best kind of bread—and then cover that with tangy tomato sauce and gooey cheese. It's the best thing ever."

Asher's face seemed to brighten as I described the food. But at the end of my description, all the pizza sat like a lump of uncooked dough in my stomach as I contemplated Asher never getting to experience things like food ever again.

We walked in silence. My feet crunched on the paved lane between the houses. Seagulls cried as they circled above. The scent of sea salt tickled my nose, reminding me the ocean was still near, even if I couldn't see it.

When we reached Daphne's white picket fence, Asher reached forward. Chuckling, he shook his head. "Sorry, my instincts kicked in. I haven't been on a walk with a lady since I was alive." His chest heaved up and down in a sigh.

My lips tipped up at the corner. I didn't prefer people paying attention to me, but having Asher call me a lady gave me an odd flutter in my stomach that I didn't hate. I opened the gate and walked through, careful not to hold it open for him in case that would look odd.

As we reached Daphne's front porch, I realized Asher's body appeared hazier, more ghostly. The farther away from his home and the places he'd frequented when he was alive, the more translucent he became.

I was about to comment on this when the front door swung open.

"Why, hello there," Daphne said. "Imagine finding you on my porch."

I hadn't even knocked. "Oh hey, Daphne." I blinked in my surprise.

From beside me, I saw Asher moving his hands in a circle to encourage me to keep talking.

Shoving the tea offering toward her, I said, "I wanted to apologize for not being friendlier earlier when you stopped by. It was a little overwhelming to be back in my grandma's house after so long. It wasn't about you."

Was it me, or did Daphne's green eyes sparkle a little at my mention of family troubles?

"Thank you." She took the bag and waved her free hand in my direction. "Don't you worry one second about it." Then just as I hoped she would, she added, "Would you like to come in and talk?"

I tilted my head forward. "I'd love that."

Daphne stepped aside to let me in, and I shot Asher a quick wink while she had her back to us closing the door.

Her house was bright, clean, and could've been in one of those beachy decor magazines. There were shells on almost every surface, rope covered trinkets, anything that could be made from sea glass was, and the walls held signs that said things like, "Life's a Beach" and "This Way to the Beach."

"Can I get you something to drink?" she asked, gesturing for me to sit on a white and blue striped sofa that looked out at the water.

Wanting to get straight to the questions I had for Daphne, I declined. "No, thank you." I plopped onto the sofa, and Asher settled next to me.

Daphne set the bag of tea on a side table. She sat on a wicker chair with a crab pillow and clasped her hands in her lap. "So …"

Scratching at the side of my nose, I said, "So."

How can I jump into a conversation like my grandma's murder? I wondered, wishing I'd planned this out a little better with Asher before coming inside. We should've been discussing a plan of what to ask her instead of the merits of pizza on our way over.

"How long have you lived here?" I asked after a long pause.

I couldn't look over at Asher without seeming completely crazy, but I felt the disappointment radiating off him.

Daphne smiled politely. "I inherited this house from my father about ten years ago."

I remembered the older man with the kind, wrinkly eyes and weatherworn skin. "Oh, I'm sorry to hear that." My cheeks colored. "I mean—not sorry that you have this house, just sorry he's not around anymore."

"Thank you," she said, but those two words were all she offered.

Her feet shifted under her and she watched me. I became excruciatingly aware of the silence, of the fact that she expected me to carry this conversation.

When she tapped her foot with impatience, I panicked and blurted out, "On second thought, I'll take you up on that drink."

Daphne got up after asking me if I'd was okay with water. Once I'd answered that I was, and she left the room, I turned to Asher.

"You said she was chatty," I whispered. "This is not chatty."

He opened his hands. "Usually she is! Your grandma couldn't ever get her to shut up."

"Then why isn't she saying anything now? She invited me in to talk. I figured she'd have a list of questions for me.

How do I broach the subject of my grandma? Do I just come out and ask her?"

Asher exhaled. "Honestly, I'm stumped. In my experience she would've spilled all the information already. Maybe it's because she doesn't know you that well."

That sentence made a light bulb flip on in my brain. Sally, a librarian at work, came to mind. "Wait. I might not live in a small town, but one of the librarians where I work is a huge gossip. I've observed her. If someone doesn't give her any information first, she'll barely tell them her dog's name. But once they share a secret of their own, she'd tell them the nuclear codes if she had them. Information is currency with people like Sally and Daphne."

Lips pursed, Asher appeared rather impressed with me. "Okay, do you have something to give her, then?"

I reflected back to the way Daphne's eyes had twinkled when I'd mentioned it being hard for me to be back at my grandma's house. I nodded.

Daphne bustled back into the room, carrying a glass of water. "Here you go, Rosie."

"Thank you." I smiled up at her as I took the drink. "I have a weird favor to ask."

Daphne's face lit up. She took her seat in the wicker chair once more.

"Well, as you may know, my mother and I were estranged from my grandma Helen," I started.

Daphne said, "We'd figured as much, since you two never came around anymore."

The *we* she mentioned must've been the rest of the residents of Pebble Cove. Daphne hadn't lived here back when I used to visit, but I'd bet many of the locals were the same.

It felt odd to explain such a large part of my life as if it were simply any other story, but I didn't have another plan.

"When I was nine, my dad—Helen's son—and I were in a car accident."

Memories of my dad bombarded me in the best way. My quiet, serious father who spent almost every waking hour hunched over his grand piano, making heart-wrenchingly beautiful music. My silly, kind father who covered my small hands with his ridiculously large ones as he taught me to play, singing each of the notes. I swallowed the lump of emotion, making it hard to breathe.

"Dad didn't make it," I said, my voice breaking. "I almost didn't either. The medics say I officially died for about a minute. They saved me."

Daphne gasped. "Oh my. I'm so sorry, Rosie. Helen told us her son had passed, but she didn't talk about it a lot."

I gazed out the window for a moment. "Grandma took the loss of her son hard as one would expect. And so Mom and I overlooked it when she started acting a little weird. About a month after the accident, she started mentioning how she hoped Dad would visit her as a ghost. She became obsessed with spirits and ghosts and thoughts of the afterlife."

"Ah, I see." Daphne smiled sadly. "So you and your mother distanced yourselves from her because you thought she was crazy. A few of the locals said that must've been it."

Gulping down a retort about how I wished they wouldn't assume things about other people's lives, I decided it was more important to correct the misconception.

"No, that wasn't it. In the accident, I broke a few bones and had to spend a lot of time at the hospital between checkups and getting casts put on, taken off, and all the rest. Mom became more tired. She quit her job as the library director at Portland State and got a job at the county library so she'd be closer to me if I needed to be picked up from school. Her patience with Grandma dwindled." I swallowed, knowing that wasn't the end of the unpleasantness. "A few months later, when my bones healed, my white blood cell count remained high. Where it had made sense after my accident, the doctors couldn't see a reason for it to be that elevated any longer. So they ran some bone marrow tests and found I had childhood leukemia."

Asher leaned closer to me in my peripheral vision. He put his ghostly hand on mine resting on the couch cushion, and even though I couldn't feel his touch, the gesture gave me strength. While it had been hard at first, now the story flowed like an open faucet.

"Mom and I jumped right into the treatment plan. She told me I would beat this: I had to since I was all she had left. When we saw Grandma Helen next and broke the news to her, Mom figured it would be the harsh dose of reality she needed to move on from Dad's death and deal with real life."

"I'm guessing that didn't happen?" Daphne asked.

This time Daphne's guess was correct. "Nope. Grandma told Mom she was making a huge mistake by putting me through the radiation therapy. She knew of a few holistic remedies she was sure would work for me instead."

I pretended to stare out the window, but actually I wanted to see Asher's reaction. He cringed and shot me a sympathetic look.

"Mom snapped," I said. "She was tired and grieving and worried, and she told Grandma it was the last straw. We never talked to her again after that. I hadn't even seen her name in over a decade before I got the letter from her lawyer last week."

I blew out a long breath.

Daphne, eyes shining, tsked. "I'm so sorry. What a

terrible mistake. One she had to deal with for the rest of her life."

"I wish I hadn't let it go that long." I pressed my lips into a line. "It's part of the reason I came over. I wanted to ask you some questions, if you don't mind. I feel terrible that I wasn't here for her funeral. Do you know who put it on? Who attended? Anything you can tell me would be helpful, would help make me feel like I was there."

"Of course, Rosie." Daphne wet her lips. "Let's see … well, Althea Pine put it on for her, of course." She tipped her head to one side as if I should know why. "And the whole town was there. In a place this small, if you don't go to someone's funeral, people might assume you're the reason they're dead." Daphne chuckled, snorting at the end.

Her words didn't hit me as funny, however. I glanced over at Asher, who studied the giggling woman.

"So the entire town?" I asked.

That had to be upwards of three hundred people if the sign on the way into town was correct.

Daphne wrinkled her nose. "Well, Carl didn't show, obviously. But everyone else was there."

My blood pounded in my ears as I put Daphne's last two statements together. *If you don't go, people might assume you're the reason they're dead* and *Carl didn't show.*

"Ask who was in the back of the room," Asher said.

It made me jump, but I remembered how much he'd been talking in the teahouse when Daphne was there, without her hearing.

"Can you tell me about where people sat? Like, who was right up front, and who was in back?" I fiddled with a ring on my thumb as I focused on Daphne.

"Well, I was up front with Althea, so I didn't see much

of the back, but the only person I'm sure was back there was Sam Hoff—sorry, I guess it's officially Mayor Hoff now."

Having had the not-so-pleasurable experience of meeting him already, I kept my thoughts about him to myself.

Daphne took my silence as confusion. "He's the new mayor as of last week. Your grandma Helen led the opposition to his campaign."

Ah. Now the political signs and his reaction to them made more sense. "She didn't like him?"

Daphne chuckled. "She didn't want any person to be mayor."

"Sorry?"

"Our Mayor Meow passed away, and she headed up the 'Keep Our Mayor Furry' campaign."

"Mayor Meow?" I felt like I was just repeating what Daphne said.

"Until a few weeks ago, Pebble Cove's mayor was a cat."

I blinked. My grandmother had been murdered, a body washed up on the shore, and now I learn their mayor was a cat? What kind of place was this?

Whatever it was, I would get to the bottom of my grandma's death. Telling our story again made me realize that while we may not have gotten a chance for closure, I could at least do this one last thing for Grandma.

7

Asher and I left Daphne's house an hour later.

She filled us in on the whole mayor saga—how it had been a close run between Meow and Jack the golden retriever about a decade earlier, but Meow had won by a whisker.

Yes, she said whisker.

A large contingent of the town loved the figurehead-type mayor, felt it placed more power with the council rather than one person. Especially for such a small town, they didn't need a mayor for much anyway. According to Daphne, the idea of keeping a four-legged figurehead gained popularity at the end. But Grandma Helen had been the real fire behind the opposition, and it fizzled with her death. They had sworn in Mayor Hoff shortly after.

"So we have a grumpy, disgruntled neighbor who hated my grandma, and a politically motivated candidate who wanted her out of the way," I recapped with Asher as we walked home.

He ran his thumbs along the inside of his suspenders. "Told you Daphne would give us some leads." He glanced over at me. "It was brave of you to tell the story about your family, to explain what you went through."

I pulled at the hem of my sweatshirt. "It is what it is. I've learned long ago that I can't change the past."

"So what does your mom think about you being here? After hearing your story, I imagine she is rather unhappy with the situation," he said.

"She's not crazy about it. She's texted me a bunch and wants me to sell." I noticed his face wrinkle in concern. "Oh, sorry. Um, texting is this thing we do where we send messages over our phones. Did you even have phones in your day?"

Asher laughed. "Don't worry. I may be dead, but I know what cars, computers, phones, and texts are."

I smiled. "Oh, good."

We approached the tea shop's stone steps.

"I think that might be why you can see me," Asher said.

"Technology?" I asked, confused.

"No," he said with a chuckle. "Your story. You technically died. You passed over to the other side in the crash. Then you were confronted with death again with your leukemia diagnosis. I spent a lot of time by myself back in those days, but I remember seeing you here once or twice as a child, and you didn't act like you could see me then, before your accident."

That made sense. I mean, technically it made as much sense as if someone told me unicorns used magic to live as horses in disguise, but I was talking to a ghost, so nothing seemed out of the question anymore.

"Maybe. And it sounds like Grandma Helen had the sight in a way since she talked about my dad coming to visit her," I suggested. "But she couldn't see you?" I asked, stopping in front of the door.

Asher shook his head. "There were times I thought she could. She might've been able to sense me. But most people can only see the ghosts of people who they knew and loved in life. The only time she talked to me was that single instance when her spirit left her body, so she was technically seeing me as another spirit. The fact that you can see me and we never knew each other, tells me you definitely have the sight, that you could see more ghosts."

This statement made my mouth drop open. "More ghosts." I'd been so busy grappling with the existence of Asher that I hadn't even considered other ghosts. "If I didn't know you were a ghost until trying to touch you, I wonder how many others I've encountered in my life." The thought made me shiver.

I suppose I'd rather encounter a thousand ghosts than another dead body though. The memory of the man, lying lifeless in the water wasn't a mental image I would never forget.

I shivered again.

I needed some space from the beach, Grandma's house, all of it. So instead of moving to unlock the front door of her house, I stepped back.

"Actually, I think I might make a trip into town. If I'm going be here for a few days, I should have more than pizza and old cookies to eat.

Asher stuck his hands in his tweed pockets. A hank of his dark hair fell forward into his face, and I marveled at how real he seemed. Now back at the house, he was vibrant, as real as my hand in front of my face.

"You want to come with?" I asked.

He picked up his head, and his eyes sparkled with interest. "Yeah?"

I nodded. "You can tell me all about this weird little

town. I should know if we're gonna figure out what happened to Grandma Helen. Plus I would like the company." I swallowed, unsure if I'd ever said those words to anyone but my mother in my life.

"Sure. Let's go."

We turned back to my car. He paused at the passenger door.

Asher's smile fell at the corners. "How about I meet you there?" he asked, his gaze flicking toward the road.

"Okay," I said, about to ask some follow-up questions when he disappeared. A shiver wound down my spine, and I climbed into my car. He might be aware of cars, but he obviously wasn't comfortable with them. The foreboding feeling loosened its grip on me as I drove. The trip to town was all of five minutes, and breathtaking in a way I hadn't remembered.

Pebble Cove was an idyllic little town situated in a horseshoe shape around the cove. Grandma's teahouse—along with the dozen or so other residents who lived on the ocean side of the Misty Drive loop—might've had the unadulterated crashing waves and coastal winds, but the houses facing the cove had shimmering blue waters that lapped at rocky shores. The only factors tying them together into a cohesive town were the Victorian-style houses and the saltwater scent tinting the air.

I maneuvered my little hatchback around a corner and onto Cove Drive, the main thoroughfare in downtown. Though it was a coastal town, Pebble Cove didn't have hoards of tourists flocking to its streets and beaches. Any restaurants or stores downtown catered to the local fishermen and their families. It didn't hurt that it was tucked away, far from the iconic Highway 101.

The road flattened out, and I drove through the main

part of the town. The white spire of the Victorian church poked up above the rooftops of the businesses and homes. Giant oaks lined the street like beautiful bullies, forcing the townspeople to build around their gnarled trunks while giving their stretching branches a wide berth.

I parked in the local free lot next to the marina, which was more crowded than I'd expected on a random Thursday evening. The sounds of seagulls mixed with the twitter of songbirds from the large oaks when I stepped out of the car. The lazy lapping of the tide moving in and out of the cove replaced the sound of crashing of waves at Grandma's house. And whereas stone and sand surrounded Grandma's beach house, her well-kept garden, the only surviving green in sight, plant life flourished in the protected cove.

Asher leaned against one of the large oaks as I got out of my car. As he'd been in Daphne's house, he was much more ghostly here in town. And while I could technically see through his body now, it didn't change the magnetism of his smile as I approached.

"So this town was all here when you were alive?" I asked as I walked over to him.

Asher nodded. "My parents were some of the original founders in the late 1880s." He chuckled. "Honestly, it hasn't grown much since then. Updated, sure, but it's remained pretty small. The locals fought about whether or not to cater to tourism but stayed a fishing village instead."

I remembered Grandma talking about that. I'd never met my great-grandpa Richard, but Grandma talked about him often, smiling over at the large picture she had hanging on the wall in the hallway. The black and white picture had shown a smiling man on a fishing boat, looking as if the sea air and salty waves were akin to a life force.

Asher waved a transparent hand in front of me. "Lost you there for a second," he said.

"Sorry, thinking about my grandma again."

He ran the heel of his hand along his jawline. "No need to apologize. You know, I spent quite a lot of time around her … if you ever want me to tell you stories." His eyebrows lifted with the offer.

"Thank you." Warmth spread through my chest. I definitely wasn't ready for that, but it was nice to have the option.

I started walking toward the businesses, my stomach reminding me once more of my lack of a proper meal in so many hours. As we walked, I spotted a large tabby cat strutting down the sidewalk, straight for me.

"Well, hello. Don't you just look like you run the place?" Bending down, I held my hand out to pet him.

"That's because he does, or used to. That is Mayor Meow, well, his ghost." Asher stepped up beside me as the former cat mayor jumped up to headbutt my hand. His head drifted right through my hand, leaving behind it a chill.

"This is the mayor?" I asked, pulling my hand back.

Like Asher had back at the house, Meow appeared as solid and alive as any cat I'd ever seen.

A couple walked by, and I stood up straight, aware that I was talking to a ghost about a cat ghost, and of our group, I was the only visible one. Chief Clemenson already found me suspicious. I didn't need the whole town thinking I was a wacko, especially not if I had to stick around for a little while.

Former Mayor Meow blinked up at me, his emerald eyes glinting in the sun. He looked far less surprised that I could see him than Asher had. Though, to be fair, he'd been dead a much shorter span of time.

Something Asher had said earlier clicked into my brain and I gasped.

"Wait, you said a soul only sticks around if it has unfinished business, if it's in turmoil." My forehead creased as I turned to Asher, checking that no one else was in earshot to hear me talking to myself. "Did someone murder Mayor Meow?" I whispered.

Asher's shoulders relaxed. "No, from what I heard, the little guy was twenty. He died of old age. Cats are different though. Their souls are much … slipperier. They can slink around a lot easier than humans. I'm guessing this guy doesn't want to stop living his glory days."

The cat regarded Asher and sniffed. He swished his tail and then walked away with the same amount of sass he had on his approach.

Smiling as the cat left, I turned to Asher. "I think you just got the cat equivalent of a bad word," I said as a woman walked by, glaring at me like I was full-on crazy.

In any other circumstance, I would agree with her worries about me. But Asher and Meow were so real to me I couldn't help it. I tried to save the situation and softened my expression, but the woman had already walked away from me.

Great. I'd spent my childhood being the girl everyone pitied only to grow into the woman they all thought was crazy.

I turned toward the grocery store. Calling it a grocery store was generous. Did it have edible food? Yes. Did Wallace, the owner, change up the items he stocked based on what local farms and artisans were selling? Absolutely. At least, that was how it had worked when I was younger.

The Cove Grocer appeared just the same as it had in my memory. Well, except the words "and Law Services" that had been added next to the original sign. Other than that, it felt like stepping back in time. The addition to the sign wasn't really a surprise either since Wallace had been the one to send me the letter a week earlier as my grandmother's lawyer.

Pushing through the door, a loud jangle of bells announced our arrival—well, my arrival. Asher walked next to me as if everything were normal, but the fact that I could see through him to the oddly stocked shelves reminded me he could've passed through the door without opening it.

All eyes turned to us—er—me.

"Oh! What a treat," a woman said as she stepped out from behind a display rack that held fresh fruit and a few handmade pies.

I observed her, waiting for signs of sarcasm. Was she genuinely happy to see me? I didn't recognize her one bit.

She approached me, hand outstretched. Her silvery hair had been braided and fashioned into a bun at her nape. She wore a cotton T-shirt and a fleece vest on top of worn khakis. She looked like the quintessential Pacific Northwestern woman. Between the rosiness in her cheeks to the warmth in her voice, I relaxed.

"You're Rosemary, right? I'm Althea Pine. I was a friend of your grandmother's."

Daphne had mentioned Althea being the one who had planned Grandma's funeral.

"Nice to meet you." I shook the hand of the woman who knew my grandma better than I ever would. All the eyes on me made me want to pull my shoulders up to my ears and hide.

"What a treat," she repeated, taking me in. "I'm so sorry about your grandmother. I miss her so much."

"Is that Rosemary? Why, I haven't seen you since you were a little sprite," Wallace called over from his register. His handlebar mustache, though still waxed and curled at the ends, was specked with white instead of the rich brown it had been back when I was younger.

"I always said she would come back," an old man with wild, white hair called from the corner, clutching a jar of pickles.

"Psh. You've never said anything of the sort." Althea turned to him with an indignant snort.

"Did too!" The man's hair seemed to stand on end the more agitated he became. "This is just like when I tried to tell everyone about my run-in with the mob, that body, and the croquet mallets. No one believed me then either."

Althea tsked and said, "For the last time, it wasn't the mob. There was only one croquet mallet and zero dead bodies."

The old man pointed the jar of pickles at Althea as if it were a weapon. "Baloney!"

"That's the Rickster," Asher whispered into my ear. "He's infamous for making stuff up around here."

And even though Asher was trying to help, his whispering in my ear only added to the intensity of the moment, amping up my anxiety. I'd been doing pretty well until now on this visit, but the old feelings of being the center of attention transported me back to when I had been sick, when whole rooms of kids, doctors, adults—whoever—would turn to stare at me. They would whisper, making my skin crawl with the noise. Everyone knew about me, the sick girl.

One of the great things about living in a big city like Portland was that no one remembered anyone. This small town where all the same people lived here, remembered me from when I was little, it all became … too much. Discomfort climbed my throat in hot spiking waves.

I couldn't even look Asher in the eyes as I turned around and walked out the door.

8

"Whoa, whoa." Asher's voice softened as he followed me out onto the sidewalk in front of the country store.

I closed my eyes and leaned into the large oak standing guard between the store and the street. When I opened my eyes, a few locals walked by, peering at me, leaning close and whispering. I couldn't tell what was more upsetting: the fact that they were talking about me or that I could see them *through* Asher.

To make matters worse, I caught movement down by my feet and noticed the late Mayor Meow twisting his way around my legs.

My life was so weird.

I put up a hand, wishing I could shoo away all the ghosts gathering around me.

They're just concerned, I reminded myself as I stared into Asher's blue eyes. *Well, at least he is. I'm not sure about the cat*, I thought, glancing down at the large feline. My mom had never been an animal person, and my current apartment didn't allow pets, so I wasn't sure what this maneuver meant.

"I'm okay," I said, keeping my hand in front of me like a stop sign.

Asher chewed on the inside of his cheek as if he didn't quite believe me. Even Meow took a seat and watched me as if I were about to explode.

"You know," Asher confided, leaning in close, "when the army commissioned me as a second lieutenant, it was only because I'd graduated from university. At twenty-four I was going to be in charge of other young men's lives. It terrified me."

My heartbeat slowed as I listened to his story. Asher had said he died about a hundred years earlier, which meant he must've been talking about World War I.

"I grew up in a fishing village," he said, gesturing to the marina behind us. "I didn't grow up around guns. Heck, my degree was in English." He paced. "Needless to say, I understand the flight response."

I smiled in thanks. "My problems are nothing like war, but they still feel big." I waved at the building next to us. "This town knows everything about my grandma whereas I know next to nothing. And then it turns out that they want to learn everything about me too. It feels too close to when the teachers told my whole class about my leukemia while I was gone at a doctors appointment, and they all stared at me when I returned."

Asher nodded but stayed silent.

"Or maybe I've gotten so used to my quiet life, checking in books at the library behind the scenes, so I don't have to interact with people." I cringed as the truth hit me. "I haven't been living the life I fought so hard to keep when I was younger.

Asher's lips twitched like he'd gotten an idea. "What if they weren't the only ones who knew everything …?" He cocked an eyebrow. "I could tell you all about them. Like how Wallace hasn't spoken to his son in ten years because of a political fight they had at Thanksgiving. Althea used to be a doctor but left her practice when she misdiagnosed a young girl. And don't even get me started on the Rickster."

The weight lifted from my chest, making it easier to breathe. "What about the Rickster?" I tried to remember him from my summers here when I was younger.

"No one knows what to believe with that guy." Asher shifted his weight from one foot to the other as he spoke.

This must be another habit left over from when he was alive, I ascertained since he weighed nothing. I chewed on my bottom lip as I contemplated this, snapping back to attention when I realized Asher was still talking about the Rickster.

"He claims to have been struck by lightning seven times, climbed Mount Everest without an oxygen tank, spied on the Russians during the Cold War, and says he married not just one, but two, famous Hollywood actresses. He also has a *guy* for any situation."

A laugh spilled out of me. The lightness it brought felt good. Well, until another group of locals walked by, and I saw the expressions of concern marring their features as I talked to myself and laughed at nothing. I needed to figure out a plan that wouldn't make me seem crazy. Okay … less crazy. At least not the concerning kind of crazy.

Asher continued, "They weren't inside, but I know a lot about the other townspeople too. Vicki is afraid the world is going to end any day and has a bunker in her basement full of canned goods. Jolene hasn't talked to her sister in three years; Henry cries whenever he hears children singing, and Christian swears he saw a UFO when he was out on his boat alone." Asher laughed.

His laughter lightened the heaviness sitting on my chest even more. "Wait … if you know so much about the town, why did we need to go talk to Daphne to get the dirt on who was mad at my grandma?" I asked, narrowing my eyes. "Why hadn't you heard about her feud with the new mayor?"

It might have been a trick of the light, but Asher appeared to be blushing. Or maybe it was just the guilty look he adopted.

He pulled in a deep breath. "I'm sorry. All of that information is stuff I've learned in the last couple weeks. Your grandmother's death shook me, if I'm being honest. I rarely enjoy being around the living—I don't even talk to other spirits." He shook his head. "I sit on the beach for weeks, float around in a fugue. I made sure I stayed current on the major things happening in the world, like technological advances, wars, scientific discoveries, but I didn't want to get involved with the drama of the townspeople or the local spirits." He paused. "Your grandma was different though. I liked her. And over the last few years I started sticking around more, started reading again —over the shoulders of her tea shop customers, of course —and I was coming back to life, so to speak. I still didn't care to learn any local gossip, but I didn't hate being around people as much. When she was killed, I felt awful that I wasn't paying more attention. Maybe I could've seen who it was or have more of a clue who did this and why. After her death, I vowed to pay more attention, to get involved. So I've spent the last couple weeks trying to catch up."

The tightness in my chest released its hold a little more. Pushing off the oak, I was finally ready to rejoin society. About a block down, I spotted Sam Hoff walking the opposite direction. He stopped in front of a building and pulled open the door.

"Hey, speaking of that sleazy mayor," I said, pointing and starting down the street.

"Rosemary, what are you doing?" Asher asked, keeping up with me.

"Last time I talked to him, I didn't know he had a motive to kill my grandma," I whispered even though there was no one near us. "Let's go question him."

"What are you going to ask him?" Asher frowned at the building Sam had entered.

I hadn't thought that far. "Questions. I don't know. I haven't planned it out. If he can show up at my house to interrogate me, why can't I do the same to him?" I walked forward, stopping in front of the building. I tapped the toes of my sneakers against the sidewalk, realizing I didn't really want to talk to Sam Hoff again. "Why don't you go in there and listen in, see what he says?" I suggested.

"Wait for him to confess to a murder we're not even sure he committed?" Asher said, shaking his head. "No can do."

"Why not? Is there a ghost code of ethics or something? Thou shall not spy on people in their offices?"

"I can't go in there." Asher pointed at the door.

The words Town Hall were etched on the glass doors.

"Are town halls sacred, like churches?" I asked. My curiosity got the better of my determined, simmering anger, and I waited for Asher's reply.

Chuckling, Asher said, "It's a new building. I can only take this form in places I visited when I was alive." To demonstrate, he held up his hand then reached out and stuck it through the door.

It disappeared.

He met my gaze. "If I try to walk in there, I'll go all

fuzzy for a while and won't know which way's up for a while before I eventually reappear back at my house—your house. It's why I couldn't ride in your car."

Turning back toward Wallace's Cove Grocer, I said, "Which means that store has been around since you were alive?"

"Yes. They've remodeled it, of course. It was Hansen's Mercantile for most of my life, but the building was the same."

"What about the abandoned cannery you talked about spending time at lately? You spent time there when you were alive?"

He stared at the store, lost in thought. Finally, he said, "Back when I was alive, it wasn't abandoned. Actually, it only went out of business about twenty years ago. It was my first job."

I pulled in a deep breath. "All right. Speaking of the store, I think I'm ready to go back inside."

Asher followed me across the street but stayed behind once we got to the glass doors marking the entrance. "I'll wait for you out here. That way you won't be tempted to talk to me."

"Good idea."

When I reentered the store, all the same people were still inside. Questions were written on their faces as they watched me, like I was a fish who had grown legs and walked inside.

"Sorry, didn't feel well for a second. Thought I might be sick." I held a hand to my stomach and puffed out my cheeks. "I'm good now, I think." I smiled.

They turned away, confirming that the skills I'd learned to get people who were worried about me to not fret were still intact.

Grabbing a basket before anyone decided they needed

to talk to me again, I scooted down a row of shelves. The shelves were tall, almost too tall. In fact, they were old and teetery enough that I worried they might crash down on me at any second. I'd picked the cleaning supplies and food storage aisle to walk down, full of things I didn't need. So I gripped my basket and headed down toward the back of the store where I could see a dairy refrigerator.

I focused on getting a few essentials. Not having Asher there helped, yet I missed his presence next to me. Wallace grinned at me as I brought my basket up to check out.

"So you're staying, then?" he asked carefully as if I might throw up at any moment.

I regretted lying about why I'd fled, but the truth was so much worse than everyone thinking I had a stomachache.

Had he heard about the dead body? The fact that I was a suspect in the man's suspicious death? If he had, he didn't let on. In fact, he genuinely seemed interested in whether or not I would stay.

"For a little while, at least," I said as he scanned my purchases.

"I know the locals would appreciate the teahouse staying open," he said, pausing to read the label on the bread I'd bought, as if he'd never seen it before. "It was a bit of a sell at first, a bunch of weathered fishermen getting dragged out to sip at hot leaf water with their wives, but Tea by the Sea has grown on the town, and a great many people would miss it."

My eyebrows rose as I reflected on this. I hadn't considered keeping the teahouse open. For one, I'd had tea for the first time in years earlier today and didn't know a thing about it.

I forced a smile. "Gretta told me there's an offer to buy,

which includes the business …" I trailed off, still unsure what I would do with the pending offer.

"Oh, that would probably be our Jolene, I'd bet," he said. When I gave him a questioning frown, he added, "She owns the Pebble Cove Tea Company down the road."

"There's another tea shop here?" I asked. "Can a town this small support that?"

Wallace touched the tip of his nose with his pointer finger. "Let's just say, her place definitely isn't half as packed as your grandmother's was." He placed my last item in the bag he'd been filling.

As he told me the total, and I paid, my mind raced with wonderings. Was this Jolene person another possible suspect? Would a person kill over a tea shop?

Grabbing my bags, I headed back outside to meet Asher. He sat by the same oak tree I'd left him next to. Meow sat by his side, and Asher chatted as if they were having a conversation.

"Can he understand you?" I asked as I approached.

Asher shrugged. "I'm not sure. He seems to." With that, he stood and waved goodbye to the cat who yawned and slunk off into the road as a car rolled by.

I almost yelled out but caught myself at the last moment as the tires passed right through the ghostly cat. My hand clutched to my chest, protective of my racing heart.

"I'll see you back at the house, I guess," I said, hoping Asher hadn't caught my mistake.

He gave me a salute and then vanished.

As I drove home, I reminded myself to talk to Asher about this other teahouse woman, Jolene. But as I pulled into the long driveway leading to my grandmother's house, all thoughts of the possible teahouse-owning suspect fled, to be replaced with my most viable suspect.

Cranky neighbor Carl stood to the side of the driveway, clipping at the hedge separating his yard from the easement. When he heard the crunch of the tires on the loose gravel road, he glowered over at me.

And even though I kept my focus straight ahead as I drove past him, I caught sight of him storming over to me in my rearview mirror when I parked. My heart jumped into my throat.

9

Although I exited the car as fast as I could, I still had the grocery bags in the back to grab. I either had to abandon them and run into the house or face the man approaching me. I decided my groceries were more important and stood my ground as I went to open my trunk. Carl's boots crunched in the gravel as he stomped over. He looked to be somewhere in his seventies.

"Hello," I said, trying to sound friendly.

"I don't need your hellos," he said, his voice menacing for how calm it was. There was a scratchiness to his tone that made me suspect old fisherman's wool lined his throat. "What I need is to know is whether or not you plan on continuing the circus your grandmother had going in that house of hers."

I jerked my head back at his gruff reply. "The tea shop?" I asked, unsure if anyone, in the history of the world, had ever before referred to a teahouse as a circus.

He harrumphed by way of an answer.

"I'm not sure if I'll keep it. But even if I sell, the new owners might keep the shop going," I said.

"Not if I have my way. You do not understand how much I hate people driving up and down this driveway past my house at all hours of the day," he grumbled.

I almost rolled my eyes but thought better of it. Seriously, though, *all hours*? The tea shop had normal business hours posted.

"You selling would give me a chance to write up a new rental contract for this easement, making sure the new owner wouldn't be able to run a business out of that house."

I scoffed, "As if anyone would sign a contract like that. Did you try to get my grandma to sign something?" I asked, digging for information about their combative relationship.

"That woman wouldn't listen to reason if it came up and slapped her in the face. And she had the original contract, so my hands were tied." He huffed.

"And so the only way you saw out of it was if she died." My eyes narrowed as I closed in on the real truth of the matter.

Carl leaned forward. "What are you getting at, young woman?"

I swallowed, steeling my resolve. It wouldn't help me to come right out and accuse him. Asking him for an alibi would also be weird since, at the moment, everyone but Asher and me assumed she'd died of heart complications.

"I heard you didn't come to her funeral," I said, finally.

Carl's expression hardened, confirming he got the implications hidden within my statement. He exhaled a dry laugh. "Yeah, well, neither did you, so …" And with that turned his back to me and walked away.

Swallowing a frustrated growl, I opened my trunk and grabbed my groceries. My overnight bag was also in the trunk, so I slung that over one shoulder.

Inside, Asher watched me surprised as I stomped into the kitchen.

"Bad drive?" he asked, shooting me a sidelong glance.

"The end of it." I let my bag of clothes fall to the floor then set the bags of food on the kitchen counter and started putting the groceries away. "Ran into Curmudgeon Carl out there." I jabbed a thumb toward the neighboring house.

Asher ran a hand over his jaw. "And I'm guessing it didn't go well."

I scowled at him for a moment before remembering he wasn't the one I was mad at. "No, but he basically told me he hated my grandmother's tea shop enough to do just about anything to get rid of it, and the only way he could get out of their current easement rental was for her to die."

"I'm not surprised to hear that," he said. "Those two had weekly yelling matches across their lawns."

Crumpling up the empty grocery bags, I tossed them under the kitchen sink where Grandma used to keep hers. I set the fruit in a bowl on the counter, turned on the heat under the kettle, and sank forward, resting my elbows on the tile countertop. My thoughts returned to Wallace's question about me keeping the shop open. I hadn't been a tea person before, but the fact that I'd started water for a cup instinctually after a bad day highlighted how much that had changed.

Returning to explaining my confrontation with Carl, I shook my head. "When he talked about her he had such hate, such disgust in his voice."

Asher waited as if he perceived that wasn't all.

After a moment, I added, "And he criticized me for not being at the funeral which is becoming something of an Achilles heel for me in this whole 'trying to avenge my grandma' idea."

"You're doing all you can now," Asher said.

I exhaled but didn't feel any better. The kettle whistled, so I turned off the heat and began making myself a cup of tea, opting for a single bag instead of a full pot of loose leaf tea like Asher had shown me how to make.

"Want me to go next door and poke around a bit? See what I can find?" he asked.

I stopped what I was doing to cock an eyebrow at him.

"I may not be able to go into the town hall building," Asher said, "but I spent plenty of time at the neighbors' houses growing up."

That was right. He had gone inside Daphne's house, no problem.

Thinking it over for a moment, I said, "What are you going to find? A note that says, 'I did it'? Honestly, we don't even know what we're looking for at this point." I sat down with my mug of tea waiting for it to steep.

Asher tipped his head to one side. "I don't have to look for anything. I could do some light haunting." At this he wiggled his fingers at me.

I narrowed my eyes. "The finger thing makes me think you don't know what you're doing."

"Psh. I've haunted people before," he scoffed. "A board creaking here, leaving a door open there …" his eyes lit up as he seemed to think of another, "closing a door that was open when there's no wind around."

Chuckling, I said, "No, that's okay. I would hate to impart that kind of terror on the man, as much as he may deserve it. Why don't we go over the clues again? Maybe we'll see a way forward after that."

Sitting across from each other at the small kitchen table, Asher and I went through the clues while we waited for my tea to steep. Asher explained, again, how he'd been on the beach and had noticed a shadow leaving the house. I tapped my foot as I listened.

"Okay, so we've got the shadowy figure," I said, standing to pull out the tea bag once four minutes had passed.

I tossed it into the compost bin on the counter before rejoining Asher at the table. Settled back in my seat, I sipped my tea while I let my mind steep in the clues.

"We've also got the campaign she was running against a human mayor," I added. "Aside from that, Carl has reason to kill her, and he lives next door so he would be close enough to sneak inside."

Asher scratched at the side of his nose. "Though it doesn't quite make sense why he would do something now instead of the last decade since your grandma opened the shop."

"True." I pursed my lips to one side, wishing I'd gotten into mysteries at some point in my reading career.

I'd always preferred happy, fun stories where the worst thing to worry about was whether or not the two main characters would fall in love, not intense things like life and death. But now that I found myself solving a real life mystery, any guidance would've been nice.

"And while the new mayor has a reason to want Grandma out of the way, we're not sure if he was even in this area that night." I tapped my fingers on the table. "Plus killing a person over a small town election seems intense."

Asher sighed. "Yeah."

Slumping back into the seat, I let my shoulders sag.

"So how long are you going to stay?" he asked, worry etched in the fine lines visible on his face.

"That's up to Police Chief Clemenson. Beyond that, I'll run out of money if I don't go back to work soon." I cringed, thinking of my tiny basement apartment in Portland—my tiny but still expensive apartment. I inspected the kitchen and tugged at my sweater.

"You could stay here, run the teahouse," Asher said.

"I don't know the first thing about tea," I said, glancing down at the mug in my hands that argued otherwise.

"I could teach you that. I listened to your grandma and watched customers enough, I could show you."

"Was her business even profitable?"

"I think so. I'd have to go through her books, but she owned the house and lived a simple life, so there wasn't much to pay for."

"But I have a life in the city." Even as I said it, I knew it wasn't true. Heat crept into my cheeks. "I-I'm going to go call my mom," I said, getting up and walking away before Asher responded.

On my way out of the room, I stopped at my bag and dug around in a pocket until I pulled out a hair tie. The coastal winds had done a number on my long hair. It felt glorious to pull it up into a messy bun.

The sun was dipping below the watery blue horizon line as I stepped out onto the deck. My fingers shook as I dialed my mom's number, so I pressed the phone up against my cheek to steady it.

"Hi, honey." Mom's voice came through warm but tinged with worry.

"Hey, Mom."

"How is it?" she asked. I could tell she was trying to slip the question in nonchalantly, but there was a tightness to her words that revealed the weight my answer would hold.

I wet my lips, staring out at the setting sun glittering off the ocean. "Beautiful. I mean, you remember."

She was silent on the other end. Then she cleared her throat. "Of course I do. I'm worried about you, honey."

In that moment, I should've told her so many things: that Grandma didn't die of natural causes, how I wish I had talked to her again before she died, that I'd found a dead body on the beach, and how the dead man had known me. I probably also should've tried to explain to her how there was a ghost here and we might be friends in a weird way or how I was liking the idea of staying here for a while.

What I actually told my mother was, "I'm meeting with the realtor tomorrow. She says there's an offer on the table, for the house and the business."

I had the urge to smack my hand onto my forehead.

"Not surprising," Mom said with a smile in her tone. "That's great," she said.

And just like that, the tension left her tone. It must've transferred to my shoulders because I stiffened, feeling awful about the amount I wasn't sharing.

"Sally finally kicked out that boyfriend of hers today," Mom said, jumping into gossip about a librarian we worked with.

I beamed. "Finally."

Mom and I settled into our usual comfortable chatting rhythm after that. I told her I would call her soon once I knew more about the offer and what my time line out here would be. It all seemed innocent enough since I wasn't lying, just omitting … a lot.

But as I hung up the call, my fingers gripped tight to my phone. It was the only anchor I had left at the end of a day that had made me question everything. And the fact that I'd shared none of it with my mom—my best friend—was most concerning of all.

10

That night, I tossed and turned in the guest bed, my conversation with my mom playing in my mind on repeat. Guilt wrapped around me like a set of unruly sheets twisted around my legs.

At one o'clock, I gave up trying to sleep, draped an afghan over my shoulders, and padded down the stairs to the library. I'd left a few lamps on, and the yellow light drew me in like I was a confused summer moth searching for an anchor.

The library had been the room I slept in when we came to visit as a family. If I had an anchor here, in this house, this room was it. Skylights dotted the ceiling, and each towering wall was full of either bookshelves or windows. In the middle of the room was a large Persian rug, two wing-backed recliners, and a leather couch. On one wall there was a piano, on the other, a desk. The desk held more of Grandma's sticky notes to herself. I smiled at her reminders to make a bank deposit and to call Henry.

Asher had said Grandma's spirit wouldn't settle for a while, possibly for months or years, but I wondered if when it did, she would come back here. Asher had come back to the house he'd grown up in, where he'd spent most of his life. So that should mean whenever Grandma was ready, this would be the place she should come too. She loved it here, always saying the beach was her true home.

I walked up to the window I used to stare out of as I drifted off to sleep, wondering if the familiarity of the space might have the same effect even though I was older. In the dark of night, the white-capped waves shone in the moonlight. The constant crashing foreverness calmed my racing mind.

"Don't be alarmed."

I let out a squeak and spun around. Asher sat in a recliner next to a dim, yellowed lamp.

He cringed. "Sorry. This is my favorite room to be in at night."

I exhaled any tension that had built in my surprise. "Me too." I settled onto the old, worn leather couch and pulled the blanket tighter around my shoulders. "In fact, I think it's why I couldn't sleep up there. I used to sleep down here when I would visit during summers, staring out at the stars and listening to the waves as I drifted off."

It was odd how even a hundred feet away in the bedrooms, the waves felt so far away, their white noise muted in a way that made me long for it to surround me, envelop me like this blanket.

"I miss sleep," Asher said with a wistful smile. He glanced at the book sitting open on the table next to him.

"What are you reading?" I asked, laying my head back on the back of the couch as I let my eyes wander up toward the twinkling stars.

"The same two pages for the last two weeks," he said. "I

miss the teahouse customers. They were a group of readers, and I caught quite a bit over their shoulders."

"Oh," I said, and hopped up to flip the page for him. "Sorry, that must be awful not being able to read."

He raised his palms in a "whatcha gonna do?" gesture. "I got desperate last week and tried to use a burst of energy to flip the page of a book in your grandma's bedroom. But I put too much energy behind it and ended up throwing the book across the room and was foggy for the rest of the day."

"Foggy?" I asked as I returned to the couch.

Asher squinted. "I can technically use energy to move things, but it's hard to control and takes a lot out of me. I can't see, hear, or think straight for a period after, depending on how much energy I expend. Back when I went through my angry phases, I tumbled from one energy crash to another, floating around in a fugue in between each poltergeist-type activity. Made some of those decades go by quickly."

"I'm sorry. That sounds awful."

"It was, but now I have you." Asher's grin was full of expectation, and it settled onto my shoulders like an overflowing return bin at the library.

As if he caught the discomfort that crossed my face, he gestured to the book next to him. "If you'll excuse me though, I've been waiting to see what happens to these siblings who've all climbed into a wardrobe that leads to another world."

"That used to be my book," I said, remembering how much I loved the story.

"It's quite good," he said. "Though, I'm not sure I buy any of this magical business."

I giggled. "A ghost that doesn't believe in magic."

"Spirit," he corrected.

Between the twinkling stars visible up in the sky, the warmth of the worn couch, and the familiar comfort of being in the library, my whole body relaxed. "Would you like me to read to you? I can start at the beginning."

Asher's face lit up, and I took that as answer enough. Hopping up a second time, I plucked the book off the side table and cradled it in my lap.

The constant sound of my voice coated the room, and we fell into the story while the waves crashed outside.

I woke to warm sun streaming on my face, the sound of seagulls cawing, and the familiar weight of a book on my chest. I must've fallen asleep during my read aloud last night. Asher was no longer in the room with me.

Keeping the blanket wrapped around my shoulders, I padded toward the kitchen. But before I made it there, I caught sight of Asher staring out of the large picture windows in the tearoom.

"Good morning, Rosemary," he said without turning.

"Whatcha looking at?" I came up next to him, following his gaze across the garden and the driveway, into Carl's yard.

The man was puttering around with those same clippers, beheading flowers and lopping off leaves as if they were responsible for all of his strife.

"I don't have a good feeling about him." I rubbed at my eyes in an attempt to wake up.

Asher didn't add his own feelings. After a quiet moment, he asked, "So are you ready?" He grinned in a way that showed me how he must've looked when he was a little boy. "I told you I would teach you the tea business, didn't I?" he said when I peered at him in confusion. "In case you open back up, that is," he added with a nervous smile.

"Oh," was all I could think to say. I'd agreed to that before I'd talked to my mother, and suddenly it felt like I was deceiving both of them. "Thanks," I amended. Then I eyeballed my sleep T-shirt and flannel pants. "I might go change first, if that's okay."

He swept his arms toward the staircase like a gentleman of old. "By all means."

As I jogged up the stairs to the spare bedroom, I realized that he *was* a gentleman of old if he was actually from the early 1900s. The fact that he'd kept up with technological innovations and cultural changes had fooled me enough to forget that. But deep down, he was still an old-timey guy imprisoned in the wrong century.

Washing my face quickly, I changed into some jeans and a light sweater. Even though it was technically spring, the old house held on to the chilly nighttime air like a child clinging to a favorite stuffed animal. My feet thumped on the drafty wood staircase as I jogged down a few minutes later, running my hand along the smooth wood railing like I used to as a kid. Long hair in a bun on the top of my head, I finally felt awake and ready to take on this lesson.

I pulled up a stool and rested my elbows on the bar. "Ready."

He cringed. "Uh, this isn't a sitting kind of lesson. I teach hands-on, and unfortunately"—he held up his hands and wiggled his fingers—"I can't help, so you'll be doing the hands-on part."

"Fair enough," I said with a chuckle and got up from the stool.

Over the next hour, he taught me how to measure the tea, steep it, the different methods my grandma had used based on the different desired strengths, and finally, how she made her custom blends. As I moved behind the bar, I found more sticky notes Grandma had left herself. One even had a tea recipe written on it. I reminded myself to try that one when I got more comfortable with the tea-blending process.

Halfway through my third cup of practice tea, I'd snuck into the kitchen to pour myself a bowl of cereal from my shopping trip yesterday. And by the time I'd graduated to learning the minutiae of water-pouring techniques and leaf agitation, I was feeling like maybe I was a tea drinker after all.

I leaned back into the old chair I occupied in the tearoom and closed my eyes. We'd moved over to a table by the window. I'd wanted to take advantage of the morning sun streaming inside, the chill having never left my toes even after putting on wooly socks.

Letting my hair out of the bun it had been in all morning, I ran my fingers through it. The dark mahogany color of it matched the brown woods rampant in the tearoom.

"Your hair is very long."

Asher was watching me, and a tickle of heat crept into my face.

"I don't cut it often." I studied the ends, combing out a few tangles with my fingers. "When I had to lose all of it during my treatment, I became terrified it would never grow back. I should probably be over the trauma of that by now, but I still never want to take it for granted, and I've kept it long ever since."

His mouth tipped up. "Makes sense to me."

A warmth that had nothing to do with the rays of sun coming through the window spread through me. Talking to Asher was so easy. I hadn't experienced this kind of openness with anyone but Mom in so long. But he got me, listened. I felt like I could talk to him about anything.

I closed my eyes and tipped my face toward the warm rays. When I opened my eyes, Asher was doing the same.

"Can you still feel the sun?" I asked him.

He smiled sadly. "No, but I can still remember what it was like. I like to pretend sometimes."

I trailed a finger around the rim of the toasty mug I clutched. "You mentioned yesterday that ghosts rarely remember the time surrounding their death, that they don't know how they died." My gaze flicked up to his. "Does that mean you don't know how you … died?" I asked.

He ran a hand over his stubbly chin. "Nope. The last thing I remember is that I was an officer in the army, and I was getting ready to meet my unit and deploy over to Europe. I can only guess I was killed in battle. Death in a war is valiant, something to be honored. I guess I'm not worried about why I'm still here because of that."

"But then what's your unfinished business?" I regretted the question. Like the man hadn't probably spent the last century wondering the same thing. If he knew, his spirit would've moved on. "Sorry," I added.

"It's okay." He looked outside for a moment. "Honestly, I have no idea. By the time I became aware I was a spirit, my family had sold this house and moved away. I tried to find them, but as I've told you before, if I travel places I never visited when I was alive, I simply end up back here."

I tapped my fingers on my lips as I thought. "And there were no clues in the town about what had happened to you?"

"Nope." It wasn't as if Asher looked upset, but the way he said the word felt like a bookend to our conversation.

Stretching, I stood. "Okay, well as much as I'd love to sit

around and sip tea all day, I've got to go visit Grandma's realtor, Gretta, and figure out what I'm going to do about this offer on the table."

Asher opened his mouth, but then he clamped it shut. His gaze flicked over the evidence of our tea-tasting lessons. Even after spending less than twenty-four hours with him, I could tell he wanted to ask why I would need to talk about the offer since I'd decided to stay.

But I was glad he said nothing because I didn't know what I was going to do anymore. If I stayed, I would disappoint Mom. But if I left, Asher would be all alone again.

My heart ached in my hollow-feeling chest. I scurried over to the bar, gathering mugs in my arms. I was rushing, but I needed to get out of there. I didn't notice one of the mugs slipping through my arms until it was too late. I didn't have a free hand to reach down and catch it.

Asher's wide eyes met mine for a split second. Then he was there, next to me. There was a whoosh of energy, and I felt the mug push back up into the space it should've been nestled in between my arm and body. I clamped my elbow tight, making sure it was secure this time.

If I hadn't been holding an armful of teacups, I think I would've fallen over from the shock. I'm not sure how anything still surprised me after a day of hanging out with a ghost who was helping me solve my grandmother's murder, but this did.

"You moved it." My words came out in a breathy whisper.

Asher gave me that same boyish grin as earlier, but then his whole body paled as if someone had turned a dimmer switch down on his spirit. "And there we go," he said, but it was much quieter, slower, more ghostly sounding.

"What's happening to you?" I asked, and as the words

left me, I remembered him talking about moving the book last night and how expending energy made him foggy for a time after.

He shrugged. "I couldn't let that mug fall." His quiet voice sounded so foreign. "It was your grandmother's favorite."

"Thanks," I said, heart aching.

He waved a slow-motion ghostly hand in my direction. "You were heading to town. Go ahead. I'm going to be fuzzy and no fun now, anyway."

I studied him for a moment, torn in the worst way. Finally, I said, "Thanks for teaching me all of that."

He shot me a quiet smile, and I left before his sadness caused me to make promises I didn't know if I could keep.

Coastal weather can change in an instant. I'd experienced it during my summers visiting Grandma.

Even with this knowledge, the gray rain clouds sweeping into the cove as I drove into town felt too much like my bad mood manifesting itself in a way that might ruin everyone else's day. By the time I parked and climbed out of the car, fat raindrops plopped onto the windshield and splattered onto my head.

I picked up the pace as I walked down Cove Drive, heading toward Gretta Montgomery's realty office. About halfway there, Meow trotted out from an alley up ahead. His green eyes locked onto mine, and his tail flicked back and forth as if it were a hand motioning for me to follow him.

I almost laughed at myself, quite sure "The cat wanted me to follow him" was sitting somewhere in the answer portion of a questionnaire to find out if you were crazy. As if the result hadn't already been a resounding "Girl, you're definitely crazy," Meow tipped his head toward the alley twice.

My eyes widened, and I stopped in the middle of the sidewalk.

"Whoops! Sorry," a woman walking behind me said as she jogged to the side, narrowly missing running into me.

Leave it to small-town people to apologize when I was the problem.

Once she'd passed, Meow waved his tail again, holding my gaze with his emerald eyes. Then he went back into the alley. Because I was now a person who saw and talked to ghosts, I checked right, then left, and followed the cat ghost into the alley.

Meow checked behind him a few times as he trotted down the cobblestone alley. His nimble cat feet jumped over puddles forming out of the rain that was now splattering down on me even though I knew he couldn't get wet. Just when I thought we would pop out into the space behind the buildings, Meow stopped and pawed at a large blue recycling bin. His paw disappeared into the plastic.

Concern corrugated my forehead. "Meow, I don't have time for games. I have to get to the realty office." I almost turned around when the cat let out a long wail.

Surprise coated my tight throat for a split second. I could hear Asher speak, so why wouldn't I be able to hear Meow … meow? The ghost cat pawed at the recycling bin again with renewed fervor.

"Okay, okay. I'll look inside." Checking that I was still alone in the alleyway, I opened the lid and peered inside.

11

I may have not read a lot of mysteries in my life, but I felt like a bonafide literary sleuth as I peered inside the recycling bin. Then, just as quickly as it came, any small sense of adventure flattened as I laid eyes on the contents of the bin.

Paper. A lot of paper.

Fat raindrops slid down my nose and splattered onto the paper as I held open the lid. I'm not sure what else I expected to be inside the bin, but that was it. Paper. I scoffed at Meow.

"Hey, man. There's nothing but paper in here. What's so great about that?"

I swear that cat rolled his eyes at me. In one floating jump, he launched his body up and into the bin like I'd seen internet cats jump into laundry baskets. His furry body floated above the top layer. He pawed at the papers. I put my hand down near him and moved them aside for him.

Satisfied, Meow sat then glanced between me and the paper that was now exposed to me. He did this a few times as if he didn't trust me to understand that this was what he wanted me to inspect.

Leaning closer, I read over what appeared to be a set of blueprints.

"The Outlets at Pebble Cove" was the title at the top of the long sheet. The next line read, "Proposal by Sam Hoff." I studied the prints for a little longer. It was a multibuilding outlet mall set up. Being that the State of Oregon had no state sales tax, these kinds of outlet strip malls were a huge tourist attraction, drawing shoppers from surrounding states who wanted a good deal.

I met Meow's gaze. "So? It looks like it's a no go since it's here in the recycling, dude. I thought you guys wanted to keep this place small, purely a fishing village. Why would you have a problem with that?" I asked him.

The cat narrowed his eyes at me. Then, in the blink of an emerald eye, he jumped out of the bin and scampered down the back of the alleyway, disappearing from sight. Mumbling something less than flattering about the feline ghost population, I closed the recycling bin lid, then I scurried toward Gretta's realty office wishing I'd brought an umbrella.

I think it was the memory of Asher's hand vanishing yesterday that made me survey the town hall building as I walked past. But it was the display in the window that made me stop. A corkboard on an easel stood propped in the window, and on it was tacked the same blueprint I'd seen in the recycling bin a few alleys down.

Well, not the same. Although the title was still "The Outlets at Pebble Cove," the next line now read, "Presented by Coastal Properties Inc." I wrinkled my nose as I read the information above the blueprints:

"Please join us at the next Pebble Cove council meeting where we will discuss the proposal to make tourism Pebble Cove's priority. Vote for a better future for our beloved home and help fulfill Mayor Hoff's promise to bring prosperity to Pebble Cove."

Rain pelted me as I stood there, and my sweater grew soggy, so I turned and jogged the rest of the way to Gretta's office. The doorbell dinged to announce my entrance, and I tucked myself into the antique chair situated in the front window.

Gretta poked her head out of her office down the hall. "Hey, my receptionist is sick today, so I'm here all alone. Come on back. I've just got to get the paperwork ready." She disappeared into the room.

I got up and followed the sounds of drawers and papers until I was in Gretta's office. While I'd talked with her yesterday, it was on the phone. The fortysomething woman was polished yet frazzled.

"Sorry," she said, puffing her bangs out of her face with a quick exhale. "I'm normally much more put together than this. Bettina being out is like losing my right arm."

Smiling over at her first to show I understood, I glanced away. I sensed my watching her was making her even more nervous. Luckily, Gretta had a beautiful view of the cove out her office window, and I got lost in the gray view as raindrops splashed onto the glass.

Gretta shoved a drawer closed with her hip. She sat down with a huff, clutching at a tan folder. "Thanks for humoring me. I was going to go crazy if I didn't put those things away."

I gave her a second to flip through the papers in the folder. "Are you excited about the outlet mall?" I asked when she finally looked up.

Gretta pressed the back of her hand to her forehead, shoving her brunette bangs out of the way. She squinted. "To be honest, I don't know how I feel about the outlets. I mean, more business is always good, but it will definitely change our quiet little fishing village." Gretta smiled uncomfortably. "Sounds like it will pass, though, so I'd better get used to it. The council's been split for years on this outlet mall vote. Mayor Hoff's already appointed three new council members known to be pro-outlet." Gretta exhaled, sending a puff of air up to ruffle her bangs. "The vote is next week."

Something bugged me about the two, almost identical plans for the outlet mall I'd seen. "What does Mayor Hoff do? I mean, other than being the mayor?"

I knew for mayors of large cities, like Portland, it was probably a full-time gig. But a small city like Pebble Cove had to be low on the mayoral duties scale, especially if a cat could've done the job for the last twenty years.

"He's in property management."

Interesting.

"So he's involved in the outlet mall buildings?" I asked, leaning forward.

"Nope. He would stand to gain too much money from the transaction. And since the outlets have been on the table for the last decade, it would seem like he only got himself elected to make sure the deal finally went through."

I sat there as if Mr. Meow hadn't just helped me uncover a potential political ethics violation. If Sam Hoff was involved in Coastal Properties Inc.—as those discarded blueprints might prove that he was—he would get a sizable paycheck bringing the outlet mall to the city. And as I'd pointed out to Asher yesterday, while a small city election didn't seem worth killing over, the potential riches an outlet mall could bring to Sam sure did.

"So ..." Gretta said expectantly. "Are you here today

because you want to accept the deal on the table?" She interlaced her fingers and placed them on top of the folder.

Pulling in a deep breath, I said, "Can you tell me more about the offer?" My conversation with my mother yesterday spun on a loop in the back of my mind as Gretta spoke.

"The buyer is a woman named Jolene Doyle. She owns the Pebble Cove Tea Company but only opened her place six months ago and it hasn't gained much traction yet."

"Can this city even support two teahouses?" I asked the same question I'd asked Wallace yesterday. This time, however, I wanted to know for financial reasons, suddenly wondering if my option to run the teahouse for income would be feasible.

Gretta nodded, pushing aside my fears. "Jolene's teas are"—she pulled a breath through her nose—"not good. She doesn't have the blending knowledge your grandmother had. She's a wonderful baker, but her tea is … awful, for lack of a better word. Other than the beautiful space, what Jolene wants most in the deal is your grandmother's recipes."

Again, killing someone over tea recipes seemed intense to me, but if Jolene's business was already failing, maybe she was desperate enough.

"And you said her offer is way lower than I could get for the place?" I asked.

"Yes, it's low even for the house, let alone with the business added in," Gretta said, her voice dropping toward the end as if she were muttering the last part to herself. "I'm sure she came in low, knowing Helen's family would counter, meet her halfway between her offer and the value estimate. I mean, I hope that's what she was doing." Gretta spun the ring on her right hand.

"Why? What would be the other option?" I kept myself from leaning in closer.

Gretta's face pulled into a grimace. "When I first got the offer, my gut told me she was hoping to take advantage of Helen's estranged relationship with her family, thinking you would sell at any price just to get rid of the memory of Helen once and for all." Her frown deepened. "Sorry to be so blunt."

I waved a hand to dismiss her worries. "It's okay. We didn't have a good relationship. You're not wrong." And while Gretta mentioning it didn't make me mad at her, if Jolene was trying to capitalize on that, it made her a pretty shady person in my mind.

"So? What are you going to do?" Gretta asked, her face softening in compassion.

Jolene's offer wasn't even remotely an option. And sure, I could meet her partway with a counteroffer, but that would still mean I would have to leave. What if it wasn't enough time for me to solve Grandma's murder? Even after everything, I couldn't leave her ghost hanging around in limbo forever like Asher.

"Please tell her I do not accept her offer," I said as I pushed back my shoulders. "I won't be selling. At least not right now."

I left Gretta's office a little while later, unsure about what I'd gotten myself into and how long finding out what happened to Grandma might take. I mentally agreed to stay here for the rest of the month. My apartment back in Portland was paid through the end of the month. My job as a book check-in clerk wasn't even a consideration, especially since

I'm pretty sure the large downtown Portland library only created the position for me because my mother worked there. They would be fine without me for a few weeks, and I would be fine without them, having saved a small amount for emergencies.

The real worry, the one that made me feel like I'd swallowed a bug before getting kicked in the stomach, was telling my mother.

I spotted Meow sitting on a bench overlooking the marina a few feet ahead. Plopping down next to him, I pulled in a deep, salty breath through my nose.

"I'm going to admit something to you, Meow. And I know it's only because you can't tell anyone or comment back, but I need to get this out … I think I like it here."

Meow regarded me with his emerald eyes, and I swear he nodded.

"It's peaceful, and I feel more like myself than I have in … since my dad died."

Meow licked his paw.

"And then there's Asher." My face flushed with warmth. "I think he might be the best friend I've had in a long time."

Meow stopped licking.

"I mean, other than my mom, of course," I added quickly. "But she has to love me, you know? And I know she still worries about me, still puts things in her life on hold to make sure I'm taken care of. Living without me might be just as good for her as it could be for me."

The cat flicked an ear back as a garbage truck rattled behind us. The sight and sound of it jerked me out of my tumultuous thoughts.

"The papers," I whispered, jumping to my feet.

Meow followed as I jogged down the street, my attention locked onto the alleyway he'd led me down earlier.

Without bringing too much awareness to myself, I picked up my pace and then ducked into the alley. If I was going to prove that the new mayor had a financial incentive to get my grandma out of the way of his campaign, I needed those original blueprints.

I skidded to a stop in front of the recycling bin. Meow stood by as I checked once more over my shoulder before lifting the lid. A gasp flew out of my mouth.

The bin was empty.

12

A heavy drop of rain plopped right onto my head, soaking into my scalp as I shivered and dropped the recycling bin lid.

"Yellow, young lady," a man said.

Jumping out of my skin, I whirled around. The man Asher had pointed out to me as the Rickster in the grocery store stood in the alley behind me. Fear prickled at my skin as I wondered if he had any connection to what had happened to the blueprints. Asher said he claimed to be a spy against the Russians at one point. He might be the mayor's lookout.

"Hi …" I croaked through the tight fear closing around my throat.

"You lost?" he asked, furrowing his bushy white eyebrows.

I gulped. "Nope, just walking through. You?"

He smacked his lips together. "Off to see a woman about a billy goat." He spun on his heel and exited the alley.

Once my heart slowed, the defeat of losing the incriminating blueprints weighed on my shoulders like a soaking-wet sweatshirt. If I didn't find cover soon, I was going to be experiencing that feeling both figuratively and literally. The rain continued to slash down on the little fishing village as I wandered the streets. I slicked my long hair back into a ponytail. It was so wet the end dripped water onto my sweater as I walked.

I couldn't even fathom going home and breaking the news to Asher that I'd lost the evidence. Not yet.

The sign hanging over one building toward the end of the downtown strip caught my attention. The Pebble Cove Tea Company. Maybe it was time to check out the competition. I jogged over, taking cover under the awning, but when I pulled on the door, it didn't budge. A handwritten note taped to the glass read Closed Until Further Notice.

Anger wound down my fingers, curling them into fists. Was she closed because she was anticipating having to sign the papers for the new business she was trying to swindle away from me? Well, that wouldn't happen. I felt like laughing in triumph.

Braving the rain again, I headed toward my car. But now the suggestion of a hot beverage sounded too good, and with Jolene's tea shop closed, I was still empty—and chilly—handed.

Luckily, I passed by a café situated on the edge of the pier, looking out at the fishing boats in the cove. The Marina Mug seemed like the perfect place to wallow for a bit while I decided what to do with my life.

When I opened the door, I expected the building to smell of sea salt and old fish given its proximity to the harbor. But the smells that hit me were that of grilled cheese, toasted bread, browning butter, and—best of all—sweet, doughy confections. It was cozy and warm inside with an iron woodstove piping out heat from the corner. Sliding into a booth close to the stove, I snuggled against the wall and contemplated the quiet harbor through the rain-spattered window.

I was the only person in the place, well, until a woman came out from the back room and strutted toward me.

"Hi there, honey," a middle-aged woman approached my table. She wore a blue apron, a wide smile, and kind eyes with lovely wrinkles at the corners. "What can I getcha?" she asked.

I ventured a glimpse at her name tag—well, the place where her name tag would've been if she wore one—but didn't see anything. There were definitely some businesses in the smaller, artsy communities of Portland that didn't require their workers to wear name tags though, so I wasn't caught too off guard.

"Hi, I'd love a hot chocolate, if it's not too much trouble."

The woman grinned at my request. "Sure thing, Rosemary. You got it."

A stiffness began creeping up my spine at her familiarity. How did she know my name?

But before she turned away, the woman leaned close and said, "I'm Vicki. We met when you were younger, but it's so nice to see you again."

Smiling, I scanned my memory. *Vicki has a bunker full of canned goods in her basement*, Asher's words repeated in my mind. My shoulders relaxed, and I sat back. He was right. Knowing as much about these townspeople as they seemed to know about me helped a little.

"Thank you, Vicki. It's great to see you."

The woman clicked her tongue and then went off to start my drink. A few minutes later she set a steaming cup of cocoa in front of me, complete with marshmallows. I wrapped my fingers around the mug and closed my eyes out of the comfort of it all.

And even though the hot chocolate was sweet and delicious when I took my first sip, I couldn't help but wish it were a mug of tea. I craved the balance of the bitter black leaves with the spices and sweetened additions. A day in my grandma's tea shop and I'd become a full-on tea person. The realization made me let out a little snort of laughter, but what started as a laugh soon morphed into a sob.

Everything I'd been carrying fell like too many grocery bags being transported from the car, ripping and spilling in the driveway. Tears spilled down my face. The emotions surrounding my grandmother's death, the opportunities to reconnect with her I hadn't taken, mixed with the knowledge that I was going to let someone down no matter what if I stayed or went back to Portland.

Luckily, Vicki stayed in the back room for a few minutes, so she didn't see me sitting in her café, crying into my hot chocolate. Unluckily, the door opened in that moment, and a flood of customers came in to escape the now torrential rain. They shook off their coats, eyed me warily, and then sat as far away from me as possible.

I sucked in my last few tears with a deep breath and pulled myself together. Controlling my sadness seemed much easier than answering questions about if I was okay when Vicki emerged from the back room, which she did a moment later to serve the new customers.

The Marina Mug filled up. Almost all the tables were stacked with people as the rain worsened. I sipped at my hot cocoa as the storm intensified outside, grateful for the safety of my warm window seat.

What is it about observing a storm from inside? There's something so wonderful about the act as if we're somehow rubbing it in the storm's face. *Look here, you can't get me. I'm enjoying this immensely, the opposite of what you wanted.*

After a few minutes, and half my cocoa, the door opened again and in stepped Althea Pine, my grandmother's friend. And just like that, those tears I'd gently folded away broke free.

Her eyes locked onto my now teary ones, and she hurried over. "Oh, Rosemary." Shaking off her wet jacket, she stuffed herself into the booth next to me and wrapped an arm around me.

Sniffing back my tears, I shook my head. "I'm sorry. I'm having a weird day, and seeing you brought it all to the forefront again."

Althea squeezed me tight. "It has to be tough."

Again, Asher's inside information about her, how she'd come out here to start her restorative center, The Pines, after making a medical mistake that ended her career, made it easier to talk to her.

"It's hard to be here, to realize that I didn't know her, or haven't for so long," I admitted.

Althea rubbed a hand on my back. Clearing her throat, she raised her voice as she said, "Pebble Cove, who has a good Helen Woodmere story they can share with her granddaughter?"

A man from across the room popped his head above the crowd and said, "Helen used nothing but tea to cure my arthritis. What are we going to do without her?"

At his kind words, more tears streamed down my face.

"Well, thanks, Joe. You just made her cry more," Althea said dryly.

The whole place laughed.

"How about some fun, quintessentially Helen stories?" Althea clarified.

"Like the time she called everyone out to Pebble Beach to help her save a beached whale, and by the time we got there, she'd already used some driftwood as a lever and pushed it back into the ocean by herself?" the Rickster called from the next table.

I hadn't even noticed him come in. After a quick glance, I ascertained there was no goat with him. The room erupted in dissent at his story.

"She did not," a woman scoffed. "That's impossible. It was the tide. When we arrived, the tide had come in and helped pulled the whale back out."

The Rickster shook his head. "False. I saw her do it."

Althea's smile widened, and my face pulled into a grin.

"Regardless of what *actually* happened, yes, stories like that are helpful." Althea glanced at my drying tears. "What else ya got?"

"Remember when she dressed in a cat suit for a full week?" a man near Vicki's counter said.

"Yes, Kyle. That was last month. We all remember it." Althea's tone was deadpan, but her face was bright with humor. To me, Althea said, "She wanted to bring attention to her 'Keep Our Mayor Furry' campaign." Althea chuckled. "And she sure did with that outfit. Looked like she could've been a cast member of *Cats*.

I giggled at the mental picture.

An older man near the back, who was a dead ringer for the picture that would come up if you typed *The Old Man and the Sea* in a search engine, said, "Two years ago, I broke my leg and was housebound. You guys remember that?"

Murmurs of agreement trickled through the crowd.

"Well, I was having a particularly bad day, and Helen called, like out of the blue, asking if she could bring me some tea and soup. She was always doing nice things like that."

People's faces softened in sadness, and I felt the tears welling back up.

"Watch it, Eric. I said funny stories," Althea warned him.

He held up a craggy fisherman's hand. "Don't worry, I'm getting to it. When she showed up, I tried to get the door, but fell. I got myself wedged between the couch and the coffee table, and I couldn't seem to get out of the spot. Helen witnessed all of it through the window in my front door. She knew I wouldn't be able to get up without her help, so she picked the lock using only the hairpins in her bun."

Everyone laughed.

"She was spicy, that Helen," a woman said.

"Fighting for good causes," another said.

"Or just plain fighting," a man added with a laugh.

"Heck, she was even fighting with Doc Gallagher the day she died," someone else said.

Most of them smiled and shook their heads like this was old news, but the part of me that knew she'd been murdered perked up at this story. To them, it was simply a fun story of how spunky she'd been until the end. And it would've been to me too, if I didn't know what I knew.

"Rain's letting up," one fisherman said, pointing outside.

The clouds were retreating, leaving a crisp evening in their wake. About half of the people downed the rest of their drinks and left money on their table, proving they'd only come in as a respite from the storm.

"Who's Doc Gallagher?" I asked Althea as the majority of them left.

"He's the retired local doctor. Doctor Ellis took over for him, but he still lives downtown," Althea explained.

Vicki came over and took Althea's drink order. "Can I get anything else for you?" she asked me.

Looking over at the grilled sandwich I saw her place in front of another customer, I paused.

"We'll take two of the grilled clubs, please," Althea ordered. "And get this girl another hot cocoa."

I let my body relax and settled in for a dinner with my grandmother's best friend.

"So why were she and the old doctor fighting?" I asked Althea.

"Who knew," she said. "It was always something new. They hated each other, flat out despised the idea of the other person. He represented traditional medicine in this town, and your grandma always had a natural, nontraditional cure for everything."

I nodded. Boy, did I know that.

"I heard about their fight that day though. It sounded pretty bad." After a moment of silence, Althea added, "I'm not sure how long you plan to stay, but I'd love it if you came up to The Pines before you leave. We have a sauna, a labyrinth, great nature trails, and even a masseuse on staff if you need to relax."

"Thank you." I wrapped my hands around my mug even though it was empty. "I think I might stay for a bit, try to tie up some loose ends. I'd love to come visit your place."

As I said this, I became very aware that the whole café had gone quiet, and most of them were listening to me. Vicki was even standing near our table, frozen with a mug of coffee for Althea. Just as quickly as it happened, the customers went back to speaking, and Vicki set down Althea's coffee.

We chatted more about Grandma over my second cocoa and our sandwiches. And for the first time since I stepped foot in her house, I felt like my grandmother was near.

But I couldn't shake the suspicion that had shivered under my skin at the way these people paid attention, listened to every word.

Was it genuine small-town curiosity, or was there a killer among them watching my every move?

13

By the time I made it back home from downtown, the sun had set. Now that I had a few hours in between me and my blunder with the recycling, it was easier to admit how I'd lost out on the clue. Asher paced through the tearoom as I explained the events of the afternoon.

"And you're sure you read it correctly?" he asked after I told him about the blueprints I'd seen in the recycling bin.

I nodded. "Positive. Meow knew what he was showing me. He knew something was sketchy."

"I guess the cat understood what we were saying, then." Asher lifted his eyebrows. "When you were in the store yesterday, I mentioned how we suspected his new counterpart in your grandmother's murder."

"Well, there you go." I held my hand out. "He dug up proof for us. Except I ruined it by not grabbing the blueprints." I mentally scolded myself once again.

Asher sighed. "Beating yourself up about it won't help. I bet Sam put them out right before the recycling truck came, for that reason. There has to be some other way to tie him to the development."

"We can only hope. Also, it sounds like this other teahouse owner, Jolene, is cementing herself as a suspect too." I filled Asher in on what Gretta had told me about Jolene's terrible tea and the low amount she'd offered for the house and business.

He ran his fingers through his brown hair as he listened. "So Sam, Jolene, and Carl all had a motive to get your grandmother out of the way."

"And when I was in town, I found out she had a huge fight with some Doc Gallagher the day she died," I said. "We need to look into him."

"She and Doc Gallagher definitely had a choppy history. I didn't need to pay close attention to town drama to see that clearly."

"But still Carl seems to have the greatest opportunity, living next door. What we need to do next is figure out where those three were on the night Grandma died." I tapped my fingers along the tea bar.

Outside, darkness cloaked the beach. My shoulders slumped with fatigue. I hadn't done much, but the emotions I'd experienced made me feel like I'd run a marathon. An emotional marathon, maybe.

"It's been a long day," Asher said. "How about we look into it more tomorrow?"

I nodded, leaving the bar and heading into the library. Asher followed. I felt the weight of the day disperse as I sank into the couch, closing my eyes for a second. When I opened them, they landed on a picture of my parents on their wedding day.

Asher must've caught the object of my focus because he said, "I'd love to hear more about your dad … if you don't mind." He settled into his favorite chair across the room.

My mom and dad had met in college, marrying after

they'd graduated. They were so young, so carefree in their wedding picture. My dad didn't yet have his signature dark beard, and Mom's hair was teased and fluffed out in a way that made her look like a different person.

"He was a pianist, but he taught music theory at the same university where my mom worked as a research librarian." Keeping my eyes on the picture of the two of them was easier than looking at Asher. "Dad was larger than life." I stopped, swallowed. But through the sadness, a smile curled at the edges of my mouth. "He wasn't exceedingly tall, but the man had huge hands and when they were on those keys, they were magic. He had a deep, booming laugh, one you could hear a room or two away."

Asher's head tipped to one side like he was resting it on the wingbacked recliner. He looked so peaceful and relaxed as he listened to me.

"Dad and I had this deal. I would go to bed without complaint, but only if he would play a song for me on the piano."

"What would he play?" Asher asked.

I snorted. "I loved all the popular movie soundtrack songs. He learned them for me. The man could play Debussy, Gershwin, and Beethoven, but I made him play the *Titanic* theme on repeat."

My focus moved to the small piano in the library.

"He loved playing in this house. Said the acoustics in Victorian houses differed completely from other buildings." I shrugged, still unsure if I believed that were true. "I kinda just think he loved this house." I studied my fingers in my lap. "It's part of the reason I want to stay. It reminds me of all the good times I had with him and my mom, and Grandma too."

When I glanced up, Asher was smiling at me.

"What?" I asked.

"I'm glad you're staying," he said then added, "at least for a little while," after I gave him a pointed stare.

A warmth spread through my chest. "I am too."

"Are you sure you don't want me to go stay at the cannery while you're here? I've been spending quite a bit of time there lately. It's something of a local ghost hangout." His forehead creased in worry.

"Absolutely sure," I said. "I've never lived with anyone other than my mom. It's kind of fun." I paused. "As long as you don't mind me being in your space."

Asher scoffed, "Do you see this?" He pointed to his smiling mouth. "I'm ecstatic to have company. Plus I made peace with the fact that this isn't my space anymore decades ago. This is your house now."

I studied my shoes for a moment. Now that I'd told Asher I was staying, I needed to tell Mom. I grabbed at my phone.

"Hey …" I said, emerging from the couch cushions I'd sunk into during my story. "I should probably go break the news to my mom. It won't be easy."

Asher stood. "Do you want some company? Moral support?"

"I think I should do this alone."

He nodded. "Okay. I'll be here when you get back."

I went to grab the mail while I was already outside. The walk up to the mailbox was long, being that it was all the way down at the end of the easement, along the main road, Misty Drive. As I walked, I fiddled with my phone, using its flashlight to guide my way in the dark. What was I going to say to my mom? And why didn't I feel like I could say it in front of Asher?

My life had gone from uncomplicated to the most complicated in a matter of days.

I twirled the end of my ponytail as I reached the mailbox. This was my mom, my best friend, the one person who'd always been there for me. She would understand. Right? I chewed on my bottom lip. Well, maybe I would leave out all the ghost stuff and the murder investigation … for now, at least. I would call her on my way back to the house.

Somewhere behind the dark clouds, the moon hid and I could barely see. Angling my phone's flashlight up, I opened Grandma's mailbox. Knowing I would have to call my mom when I finished, I stood there flipping through the mail to procrastinate. I jumped as the revving sound of an engine roared behind me.

I whipped around to see a car sitting on the other side of the road with its lights off. Suddenly its headlights flicked on, blinding me. In my surprise and confusion, I didn't hear the screech of the tires until it was too late. All I could do was turn to face my end, blinking in the bright headlights.

Something wrapped around my wrist and pulled hard, tugging me back. My mail went flying along with my phone. The flashlight strobed all around me as letters fluttered to the ground.

I thumped into a solid, scratchy object, gasping as what little air left in my lungs was shoved out. I was about to ask Asher how he'd managed to grab me when my savior coughed.

"Okay, gimme some space here," grumbled a man who was definitely not Asher.

Taking a step back, I noticed Carl standing in the light of my phone's flashlight, pointing straight up where it had landed among the pile of mail.

"Carl?" I croaked out his name. "What …?" I glanced back toward the road.

The car had disappeared down Misty Drive, heading toward the lighthouse where the road looped back up toward town. The only sign left was the dust kicked up by its tires from where they'd left the asphalt and hit the dirt shoulder near the mailboxes.

"What the heck are you trying to do out here?" he finally asked, stooping to pick up my mail.

I knelt next to him, grabbing my phone and pointing it at the ground to help us see. "Me? I was getting the mail. That car almost ran me over." I shivered, thinking about how close they'd gotten to me.

Carl's face tightened, and he dusted himself as he stood. "Well then, I saved your life. If you want to return the debt, you can leave town." He gestured in the direction the car had fled. "You obviously should if you know what's good for you, if you want to stay alive."

Narrowing my eyes, I scoffed, "Are you threatening me?"

Hand resting on his chest, he said, "I'm not, but just did. I saved you."

After a moment of contemplation, a terrible thought came to mind. "How convenient that you just happened to be out here." I scrambled to my feet. "Did you have something to do with that?"

Carl held his hands out like two stop signs clutching mail.

I pointed an accusatory finger in the older man's direction. "It is why you were out here," I said. "You planned that!"

Hands still raised in defense, his face broke into a pained grimace. "I promise I had nothing to—"

"Sure! Great!" My face burned hot with anger, and I

snatched my mail from his hands. "I *totally* believe you." I scowled at him. "You hated my grandmother's tea shop that much? Well, I'm sorry to disappoint you, but I'm staying." With that, I stomped past him and down toward the house.

Inside, Asher's face was a list of questions as I threw the crumpled mail down onto a table with a huff. The front door slammed behind me.

"Wha—" he started to ask, but I didn't even let him get the question out.

"I'm officially ready for you to haunt Carl," I said with a sweeping gesture next door. "Go for it. He's all yours. Go haunt away."

Asher cringed. "I mean, it doesn't feel like I have enough informa—" He cut off as I glared at him. He put his hands up. "Okay, here I go. Going to haunt the neighbor. Oooooohhh." He let out a long ghostly sound as he vanished through the exterior wall.

Stomping into the kitchen, I plunked the kettle onto the stove top and turned on the burner. I needed the calming effect of the chamomile tea I'd tried earlier during our practice session. Turning around, I jumped when I saw Asher standing in the kitchen doorway, his face grim.

"What?" I asked, covering my pounding heart with my hand.

"I can't haunt Carl." Asher rubbed the back of his neck.

"And why not? The man threatened me, Asher."

Asher cringed. "He's … crying."

14

"Crying?" I asked.

In the background, the kettle made a plinking sound as it warmed up.

Asher shrugged. "He's sitting in his living room crying."

Wrinkling my nose, some—but definitely not all—of my anger dissipated. "Great." I threw my hands up. "Now I feel bad for the man who threatened me after some maniac in a car almost hit me."

Asher blinked. "Wait. A car almost hit you?"

I sank into the closest chair at the small kitchen table. "Yeah, out by the mailbox, but Carl pulled me out of the way."

Asher looked confused as the kettle whistled. So while I made myself that chamomile tea, I filled him in on everything that had happened after I left the house.

"There's no way they could've known I would go get the mail this late at night, but it did seem like they were waiting for me …" I rubbed my hands up and down my arms to get rid of the goosebumps.

"You need to call the police," Asher said seriously. When

I opened my mouth to protest, he held up a hand. "Someone tried to hurt you or scare you off. Either way, that means your grandmother's killer is coming after you."

Conceding, I called the police station. It wasn't an emergency as the vehicle no longer chased me, so I expected to leave a voice mail asking the chief to call me when he had the chance.

Which made it even more surprising when he picked up.

"Chief Clemenson."

"Oh—hey! Hi, Chief. Did you—I didn't know you … answered the phone." My cheeks flushed with heat at my awkwardness. Asher hid a smile.

"Who is this?" he asked.

Right. He wouldn't know who I was. As easy as it would've been to hang up and try calling back later, he would recognize my number now. Plus it wasn't like the man thought I was normal, anyway.

"This is Rosemary Woodmere. Helen's granddaughter."

He sniffed as if he could've guessed as much. "What do you need? Finally remember how it is you know Mr. Mastronardi?"

"Uh, no. Actually, I'm calling because …" I turned to Asher for support. He nodded. "Because I almost got run over by a car."

"I don't see why that's any of my business. Stay out of roads, Miss Woodmere."

"I wasn't on the road," I said tightly. "Someone tried to hit me while I got my mail."

I don't know what reaction I had expected at this news, but the flippant "huh" I got from the police chief definitely fell short of any prediction.

"I'm heading out your way tomorrow anyway to ask you

more questions about Mr. Mastronardi. I'll take a statement about the car thing, then." And he hung up.

Car thing?

I snorted.

"What'd he say?" Asher asked.

"He'll be out tomorrow?"

Asher rolled his eyes. "He thinks you're lying again. Or he doesn't care. Either way, we're on our own with this mystery. And I have a suspicion it's linked to your grandmother's death."

I puffed out my cheeks. "So what do we do about Carl?"

"I'll admit the man's not coming out of this smelling like roses," Asher said, "with warning you to leave town and all."

I dipped my head in concession.

"But he's also not seeming like a murderer." Asher lifted his shoulder as if *not seeming like a murderer* was somehow hard and cause for celebration.

"What if he's crying out of guilt?" I ventured. "Maybe he's suffering from guilt after killing Grandma Helen? We don't know for sure he wasn't involved in the attempted hit and run. I still think it's suspicious that he *happened* to be out there at the same time."

"Carl takes nightly walks down Misty Drive to the lighthouse and back," Asher said, checking the time. "It's just about the time he's normally out there. I bet that's what he was doing."

"Oh …" The information sucked the last bit of wind from the sails of my accusation. I stared out into the dark night. "Do you think I should go talk to him?"

Why did I feel responsible for his tears? He'd threatened *me*. But then again, he'd also saved my life.

"I'll go with you." Asher held me with his piercing eyes.

I stood. "I'm taking my tea with me. That way, if things

go sideways, I can at least hit him over the head with the mug, or scald him with the boiling water."

Asher laughed. "I promise, I'd use up every last bit of my energy to stop someone from hurting you."

His confession was sweet, but also intense. I swallowed and then walked forward because I didn't know what else to do.

Outside, the crisp sea air hit me like a jolt of caffeine. The ocean was loud and dark and seemed like it called out a warning. A shiver danced down my spine, and I wished with all my might that I could reach out and hold Asher's hand to help my nerves. He smiled over at me as we walked, and I curled my fingers tighter around my warm mug.

A few moths buzzed around the halo of light given off by Carl's front porch light, banging into the bulb every once in a while. I pulled in a deep breath before knocking.

"I don't open the door after dark," came the gruff response from what sounded like right behind the door.

"Carl, it's me, Rosemary. I know you can see me." I waved at the peephole just at eye level.

"You made your feelings clear. I don't care what else you have to say." I even heard him harrumph through the door.

I planted my hands on my hips. "Look, I'm not the one threatening innocent neighbors." I turned to leave, to give up on this impossible man, but Asher caught my gaze with his and I softened. "I'm sorry for running away like I did. I wanted to come and thank you for saving me."

There was a beat of silence, but then the lock clicked open, and the door swung in.

Carl's face folded into a scowl, but interest showed in the small twitches of his lips. "Uh, okay. Well, you're welcome."

I let my eyebrows rise. "Can I come in?" I asked.

His face clamped even farther into a frown. "I don't usually invite people into my—"

My head fell to one side in exhaustion. "I'm trying to be friendly, and it's cold out here. You're welcome to come over to the teahouse, if you'd rather."

He fidgeted with the doorknob. "No, no. I don't want to set foot in that place. Fine, come in."

Whereas Daphne's house had been all whites, creams, and turquoises, Carl's was dark woods, dark rugs, and the thick presence of even darker memories in every corner. He walked me down a long hall and into a small living room attached to a kitchen. A roaring fire burned in a stove in one corner.

Black and white photographs of a young man on a fishing boat adorned his kitchen walls. The young man's smiling, tanned face was unrecognizable at first, but as the photos changed over to color, I saw Carl in the weathering features of the fisherman.

One picture of a gangly teenager standing in front of a looming concrete building stood out to me.

"What's this?" I asked, pointing to the photograph.

"My first day at my first-ever paying job." Carl jerked his head to the right. "At the old cannery up the road."

I glanced at Asher. They had that in common. The photographed teenager's face was so bright, so full of expectation and hope that it made my chest ache.

The real-life version of the man in the photos sank into one of the worn chairs around a small table in the center of the room. His bushy white eyebrows furrowed as he looked across at me when I settled into the chair across from him. Asher sat in the third, but I focused my attention on Carl. A wayward teardrop clung to the corner of his white mustache, and his eyes were red like he'd been rubbing at them.

"Is everything okay?" I asked warily. "You and my grandma had some feud going, but I get the sense her death actually upset you. Did you two have some weird love-hate thing going? You can tell me."

"The only thing I had with your grandmother was a hate-hate *thing*," he said with disdain.

Asher scoffed at the same time I did. "What's that supposed to mean? Just so you know, that sounds terrible and doesn't inspire confidence that you had nothing to do with her death."

Asher cringed, his shoulders flattening at my blunder. Shoot, I had been trying *not* to accuse him of murder.

"Her death?" Carl stuttered. "She died of heart complications."

Waving a hand, I tried to move on to another topic. "Right. Whatever."

But Carl wouldn't let what I'd said go. "No, no, young lady. What did you mean by that?" His body straightened as if he might stand up, but then he thought better of it.

Exhaling in frustration at myself, I set my tea mug on the table. "I don't believe she died of natural consequences. And it doesn't help that you two were in some mortal feud over the driveway, not to mention all the threatening things you've said about her, and now me."

Carl's gaze dropped to his hands. He fidgeted for a moment before saying, "I didn't like your grandmother, it's true." His dark eyes flashed up to meet mine. "But I would never hurt her or anyone else. The way you looked at me out there, like I was a monster …"

My posture softened, but I kept my face firm as he returned his gaze to me.

"It's true that I don't like cars going up and down the easement. I'm retired, and I want to be able to relax, not have hooligans driving by me all day."

"Hooligans? They're townspeople, other Pebble Cove residents. I hear you guys don't get many tourists out here." I crossed my arms over my chest.

He rubbed the back of his neck. "Like I said, it's not only that. Your grandmother and I haven't seen eye to eye since you left."

"Me? What does this have to do with me?"

He cleared his throat. "I don't know if you remember my granddaughter, Jenny." Despite his throat clearing, his voice still cracked around her name.

The word rang like a crystal bell in my memory, producing the image of a young girl. I was eight, and she had been probably half my age with golden blonde hair streaming behind her. The pain in his face made my chest tight with worry.

Carl covered his face for a moment. "When she was ten, she went on summer vacation with her friends to a beach up in Washington. She got pulled out. The current was too strong." Tears shone in the man's eyes. Sniffing once, Carl seemed to push all the emotion back down, and a jaw muscle tensed in his cheek. "Your grandmother tried to console me, to tell me she'd lost you too. But it wasn't the same at all. You were still alive. She could still be part of your life, but she chose not to. And for that, I could never forgive her."

His story felt like a gut punch. The fact that Grandma had told him she'd lost me was like a slap to the face. Thoroughly emotionally beat up, I propped my elbows on the table as if they might help hold me up.

"So yes, I hate the tea shop, but our feud was about so

much more than cars driving past my house." Carl studied his hands. "I apologize for the threat. It was the wrong thing to say, especially after you'd just had a scare."

My anger at him fizzled away as I took in the pain he was still in, decades after losing his granddaughter.

"It wasn't only my grandmother's fault we didn't talk," I mumbled as I inspected the tea in my mug. "She tried a few times, but my mother wouldn't let her near me. And I've been an adult for almost a decade now. I should've come to see her."

"I suppose there's always two sides to any story," Carl said. "She never told me any of that." His expression clouded over. "And you think her death wasn't natural?"

I cringed at my stupidity in blurting that out, but now there was no taking it back.

"I promise you I didn't hurt her," he said.

My nostrils flared. "Where were you on that Wednesday night? Around nine or ten?"

He puffed out his chest. "The night before they found her? That would've been the seventh?"

Checking with Asher, I whispered a hoarse, "Yes."

"At the Dragonfly theater. Wednesday nights are half-priced and they play classics."

I eyed him suspiciously.

"Look, I might seem like a hermit, but I actually go out sometimes. I have the ticket stub, and half the town saw me."

My lips pursed. "Half the town?"

He nodded. "Most of the older generations, albeit. The youngsters mostly have no interest in the classics. Even though it's a crime, if you ask me."

"What counts as younger?" I asked then amended my

question with, "Did you see Jolene or Mayor Hoff there that night?"

I'd already blurted out the part about thinking Grandma didn't die of natural causes, so what could it hurt to tell him who I suspected? Maybe he had information that would help.

Carl's chair creaked as he leaned back. "They're definitely in the too-young category. No, they weren't there. You think they had something to do with Helen's death?" Before I could answer his question, he seemed to answer it himself, realization showing in his features. "Ah, I see. The campaign and the teahouse, both motives to get Helen out of the way."

"What about Doc Gallagher? Was he at the movies?" A retired doctor definitely sounded like he fit in with the older group of residents, and I expected Carl to nod his head. When he shook it, I felt like coughing in surprise.

"Actually, Gallagher wasn't there that night. It was odd since he rarely misses it. You think he had a motive?"

I tugged at the hem of my sweater. "I don't have a ton to go on yet, but I might be close."

Carl scoffed, "I'd say you are. Someone out there sure is worried you're here." He jabbed a thumb in the direction of the road and the mailbox where I'd almost been run over.

"But why today?" I mused. "I was here all yesterday without so much as a problem."

Carl squinted. "Well, what did you do different today?" he asked.

I'd been digging around in the recycling. Had anyone seen that? And then I'd turned down the offer Jolene had made. Gretta had surely notified her I didn't accept the offer by now. Or there was the eerie silence that had followed my announcement about how I was going to stick around for a while at the Marina Mug. I might as well have broadcasted the news to the whole town.

I sucked in a quick breath. Either Jolene, Sam, or this Doc Gallagher person could've been the ones watching me, trying to run me over. Heck, maybe I'd been right about the Rickster being someone's lookout.

Regardless of who it was, it meant that not only had my grandmother been murdered, but my life was now in danger too.

15

Asher and I left Carl's house a little while later. My tea was long gone, and the mug had gone cold in my hands. We walked in the dark, lingering on the back porch as the sound of the waves crashed around us. I loved how the moon reflected off the whitecaps, making them visible even on the darkest of nights.

"So Carl didn't kill Helen." Asher's face turned toward the moon.

But the moon didn't reflect off him in the same way it did off me. It reflected off *all* of him, making him glow in the darkness. Other than when he became transparent, this was the ghostliest he'd appeared in the time I'd known him.

I exhaled. "I'm so relieved. Having a potential murderer next door was stressful."

Asher frowned. "The killer might not be next door, but they're close."

He was right, and while I'm sure he didn't want to say it aloud, there was still plenty cause to stress.

"Well, there's nothing we can do about it tonight." I

yawned. "The police will be here in the morning. Until then, I'm going to get some sleep."

Asher turned and caught my gaze with his. "I want to make a promise. I won't fail you like I failed Helen. I won't let anything happen to you."

Gulping, I wished so fervently that I could touch him, that I could pull him into a hug.

I remembered back to when I was in the throes of fatigue and bone pain during my leukemia treatment. Mom didn't want to hug me because it hurt, but she wanted me to know she was there for me. Somehow, though, Mom telling me how much she wished she could hug me felt almost as good.

So I tried it, hoping he would feel the same.

"I wish I could hug you," I said to Asher. "So much. Thank you for your friendship." I reached my hand out, but it only wafted through his.

Asher's face pulled into a sad smile. I turned to go inside, knowing sleep would be scarce after the events of the day.

The next morning, there was a knock on the front door while I sipped at a cup of tea. I spotted Police Chief Clemenson's cruiser in the teahouse's parking lot as I walked up to the door.

"Hello, Miss Woodmere," he said, holding his hat in his hands.

I gestured for him to come inside.

The police chief stepped into the tearoom, settling at one of the two seater tables. I took a seat next to him.

Asher was already at a different table, reading the newspaper I'd laid open for him. He still preferred to read his news in paper form, given that's how he'd grown up, he said. He glanced up from the newspaper and regarded the policeman with suspicious interest.

"Can I get you some tea?" I asked, moving to stand.

Clemenson held up a hand to stop me. "No, thank you. I hate the stuff. Much more of a coffee drinker." He cleared his throat once I was seated again. "So … you had an incident yesterday."

I nodded. "Someone tried to run me over last night." I pointed toward Misty Drive. "At my mailbox." Contemplating telling him about Carl's involvement, I figured it would only distract the police chief, so I kept those facts to myself.

"And what made you think they were trying to run you over?" he asked.

Asher scoffed from his table. In my peripheral vision, he shook his head.

"Uh, the veering toward me and squealing of tires kinda gave it away." I crossed my arms.

"Did you see what the car looked like?"

"Fast? It had bright headlights." I offered.

"Did you have any enemies in town, Miss Woodmere?" He scratched some information down on his notepad.

His obvious doubt made me want to scream. "No, Chief. But my grandma obviously did, and I'm pretty sure she was murdered. That person is now coming for me."

The police chief took in a deep breath and then let it go. "Miss Woodmere …." He rubbed his face. "What makes you think that?"

Knowing he wasn't asking seriously didn't stop me from giving him a serious answer. This was my chance to tell him what was going on, and I wouldn't miss it.

"Isn't it interesting that her antihuman mayor campaign

was gaining traction and then the next week—only a week before the special election—she suddenly dies?" I asked.

The chief sighed.

"Hear me out," I said, knowing the chances of that request were low. "People in town say that Mayor Hoff isn't involved in the new outlet mall plans, but how sure are you about that fact?" I stopped and shot a pointed glare at the policeman. "I found blueprints that had his name on them in a recycling bin. He was obviously trying to get rid of evidence that connected him to the project. Why would he do that if he wasn't trying to cover up the fact that he's still involved?"

Chief Clemenson scratched his nose. "And do you have proof of these blueprints?" he asked, fatigue lowering his tone.

I grimaced. "No. I saw them, but the recycling truck picked them up before I could go back and take a picture. I didn't realize what they were proof of until it was too late."

"And what do you believe they are proof of, Miss Woodmere?"

"A huge ethics violation," I said, unsure how he couldn't see the same. "The mayor says the outlets are in Pebble Cove's best interest, but what if they're not? What if all he cares about is that he'll get rich? Tell me, had anyone ever proposed an outlet mall before?"

The chief shook his head. "I mean, it was discussed, but until lately it didn't have the votes to pass in the town council."

"Because the new mayor appointed people to the council who will vote for it. And the potential riches he would gain by becoming the mayor who brought such a development to the town would be a great motivation to get an old woman out of the way if she were threatening his chance to become mayor."

The chief barked out a contemptuous laugh. "Miss Woodmere, I've known Sam Hoff his entire life. The man loves this town as much as I do. I'm sorry. I don't buy it."

Asher muttered in irritation as he continued reading the newspaper at the table across the room.

"What about this Doc Gallagher that she had a screaming match with the very day she died?" I said, knowing I sounded like I was grasping at straws now that he'd turned down my most solid lead. "That sure sounds like a person mad enough to take action."

He opened his mouth, but I didn't let him shoot it down.

"Or," I said, cutting him off, "this Jolene Doyle, who was my grandmother's competition. Did you know that she offered an extremely low offer for this house and the business before Gretta had even officially put it up for sale? That sounds like someone waiting in the wings to snatch up something she wanted. Maybe her business is going so poorly that she would kill the competition if she thought that was the only way she was going to get her hands on my grandma's recipes."

"Jolene Doyle's been in a full leg cast for the past month," he said, his words dripping in disdain. "How do you suppose she killed your grandmother when she can barely make it around her house?"

I reflected back to when I'd walked past the Tea Company yesterday. It had said *closed until further notice*. Okay, so maybe it couldn't have been her …

"Jolene aside, how did either Sam Hoff or Doc Gallagher kill Helen?" he asked, catching me by surprise.

Was he actually taking this seriously?

I pulled in a fortifying breath. "She was poisoned."

"Poisoned." He let out a single laugh. "And how do you know that?"

Of course, I couldn't tell him how I knew that—the major downside to getting your information from a ghost. I picked through options in my brain. Finally, I settled on, "What else could it be? It had to have been a poison or drug that wouldn't have symptoms too different from a heart attack. She didn't have any signs of bruising around her neck or knife wounds on her body, so the killer must've poisoned her." I blinked. "They might have tampered with the medication she took each night," I offered nonchalantly.

"Now you believe this killer is trying to get you out of the way as well?"

I lifted my chin. "I do."

"And while they poisoned your grandma, they've changed up their method to vehicular homicide for the fun of it?" He raised an eyebrow.

He had a point. Why wouldn't they try to poison me too?

"Maybe they weren't trying to kill me, merely scare me off?" I said. "Killing a woman in her eighties is a lot different than one in her twenties. Maybe they thought if I was too scared to stay here, I might stop looking into my grandmother's death?"

As I offered the suggestion, pride welled inside me. That made sense. I was getting pretty good at this sleuthing gig. Not to mention how I was standing up to the ornery chief despite my usual aversion to confrontation.

The chief nodded, catching me off guard. "I agree."

I just about jumped out of my seat in triumph.

Then he added, "It would be best if you stopped looking

into your grandmother's death. I'll take over from here. You have enough to worry about trying to sell this place." His focused expression showed me that's what he wanted me to do—leave. I could also tell he had no intention of actually checking up on the suspects I'd given him. "Now, on to my questions about Frank Mastronardi," he said.

I resisted the urge to fold my arms in front of myself in angry defiance.

"We've done a little more digging and found out he was coming to meet with you to put an offer on your grandmother's house. Are you sure you never talked to him about that?" He studied me the way a hawk studies a mouse before sinking its talons into flesh.

Keeping my chin up, I held his gaze. "Chief Clemenson, I do not know that man. I'd never spoken to him, seen him, or even heard his name before the day he washed up on my grandmother's beach. You can ask me all you'd like, but my answer won't change." I sat back.

Slow clapping came from the side of the room as Asher cheered me on. I didn't dare look over at him, knowing it would make me smile and seem crazy in front of the policeman again.

"I guess we're finished here, then." Chief Clemenson stood. "But please know I'm going to continue to dig, Miss Woodmere. And if I find out you're lying about any of that, it'll be pretty hard to talk your way out of it. This is a small city. All of my energy, and the energy of my three officers, will be devoted to this."

"When it's not devoted to looking into my grandmother's death, right?" I raised an eyebrow. "Because if you won't, I'm definitely going to continue."

Closing his eyes for a moment, he said. "Right. And

looking into that. I'll be in touch, Miss Woodmere. I can see myself out."

Once the front door shut, Asher said, "He's not going to do a thing."

I narrowed my eyes. "Nope. Which means, we're on our own."

16

A few minutes after Police Chief Clemenson left, I leaned on the kitchen counter, chewing on my lip.

"What are you squinting at?" Asher asked as he entered the room.

I glanced up. My face felt stuck in the scowl I'd adopted while trying to read on my phone's small screen. I held up my phone, opening my mouth to stretch my facial muscles back into place.

"Doing a little research on this Frank Mastronardi character."

"Find anything?" Asher sat at the kitchen table.

"I can't see anything on this." I gestured to the phone. "Did my grandma have a computer?"

Asher cringed. "Yeah, but … you're not going to want to see it."

My head shot back. "Why?"

He chuckled. "I think it might be older than you." He left the room.

I followed, intrigued. He walked into the study that attached to the library. With a flourish of hands, he gestured to a large dinosaur of a desktop computer, complete with dust as if there was any question in my mind how much Grandma had used it.

"This?" I let out an exhaled laugh. "But she owned a business. How did she take payment?"

He crossed his arms in front of his body. "She only took cash."

"Seriously? Who does that anymore?" I poked at the power button and jumped as the machine beeped and then roared to life, sounding like it was powering a small airplane inside. "Where did she keep her financial spreadsheets?"

"All by hand," Asher said, motioning to the long drawer in front of me.

I grimaced in anticipation as I pulled it out and saw checkbooks, notebooks, and old-timey financial record-keeping books. My eyes widened in awe. On top of the desk, the old computer's fan sounded like it was trying to take off, yet the screen only showed a loading sign.

"Okay, well this won't be any less frustrating." I waved to dismiss the old machine. "I wish I'd brought my laptop with me."

"There are computers at the library downtown."

The suggestion made me perk up. After Chief Clemenson left, I'd felt a little hopeless about everything we were trying to do.

"That could work." I walked out of the room and into the kitchen. "Want to come with?" I asked, grabbing my keys off the counter.

Asher stuffed his hands in his pockets. "It's a new library. I can't go inside."

"Then how do you know there are computers?" I pressed my lips into a thin line.

"I can see through windows." He chuckled.

I smiled at my oversight. "Okay, well, I'll be back soon. Need anything in town?" I asked stupidly before I realized my mistake.

To my surprise, Asher said, "Actually …"

I stopped.

"When you're at the library, would you do some research on me?" The sincerity backing his request cut me right to the bone.

"Of course!" My cheeks flushed. "Omigosh, Asher, I'm so sorry I didn't consider doing this earlier. I'd be happy to."

His once tight expression softened. "Thank you. Since my parents had left town by the time my spirit settled, and no one seemed to talk about me in town after that, I've never had this opportunity."

"Absolutely. I'll find out whatever I can."

Before I left, Asher told me the number of his regiment in the army, the number of the group under his command, and the army base they'd been sent to on the East Coast before their deployment. Armed with those pieces of information and a notebook and pen, I headed into town.

Raindrops pelted me on my way to my car from the tea shop. I pulled one of the many hair ties from around the gearshift and tugged my already damp hair into a bun in preparation. On the drive, I eyed a dark cloud that hung over Pebble Cove like a Macy's Thanksgiving Day Parade of foreboding, warning everyone to take cover. Asher had been right yesterday when he'd said the break in the rain last night might be the only one we would get for a while.

The Pebble Cove Public Library was situated across the cove from the marina, where boats didn't impede the view. I couldn't help but think how much Mom would love working here, being able to stare out at the water all day as she checked out books and helped people with their research.

As I thought about it, though, she'd probably hate how small the place was. She thrived on the size and amount of new customers she got each day in the Multnomah Central County Library where we worked. And while I loved the beautiful 1913 building with its marble columns and elaborate staircases, it had always been a little too grand for me.

This little library perched on the rocky shore of Pebble Cove, full of driftwood art and overstuffed chairs, felt like home the moment I stepped foot inside. Knowing I'd need to sign up for a library card to use the computers, I did so first.

"Good to have you here, Rosemary," the librarian said as he handed me my card. He had a real Mr. Rogers vibe going for him and made me feel confident he was glad to be my neighbor.

Or maybe it was the fact that his first name *was* actually Roger. I giggled to myself thinking of him being named Roger Rogers, but it was just Roger Foss.

Library card in hand, I headed toward the shelves. I may have had a mission, but I had to at least take a moment to browse around, to pull at least three books from the shelf and run my fingers across their coffee-cream pages. After one tour around the place, I was about to settle into one of the computer cubicles when I noticed a spiral staircase in the corner. A sign on the wall pointed upward and said, "The Loft."

Curious, I climbed the staircase, running my hand along the wrought iron as I curled upward. When my head surfaced above the floor, a smile spread across my face, only growing larger as I reached the top step.

The Loft was about five hundred square feet of reader paradise. Large picture windows ran the length and width of the second story, giving the room a breathtaking view of the cove from a taller vantage point. Cozy couches, beanbag chairs, and a meeting table filled the space. To my right, a railing looked out over the rest of the library below.

If I didn't have research to get done, I would've stayed here until the place closed. Reminding myself to come back at another time, I headed back down the staircase toward the bank of computers in the middle of the room.

I logged in after settling behind one. Knowing it might be a long shot, I typed Frank Mastronardi's name into the search engine. A few hits came up: one on LinkedIn and another on social media. I was about to click that one when something more intriguing caught my eye. The third search result was for a property development company.

I clicked the link.

After a few minutes of navigating their site and a few of the other search results, I knew three things about Frank:

1. He was a developer specializing in retail spaces, specifically strip malls.

2. He'd moved around a lot, for business. He liked to live where he was working so he was fully invested.

3. He didn't have any family or close friends.

And he was here to talk to me? I wrinkled my nose as I thought about that. Honestly, it made little sense. Sure, I had inherited some property, and maybe he was interested in it, but Grandma's beach house was nowhere close to the proposed outlet mall lot I'd seen plans for in the city-hall window.

As a developer, it made more sense for Frank to be here talking to Sam Hoff.

So many light bulbs clicked on in my mind that I felt like an employee in a lamp store preparing to open the shop for the day. What if Sam was involved in the man's death and he'd planted my name on him to take the police's suspicion off himself?

I shifted in my seat at the thought, eager to share the information with Asher as soon as possible. I was about to stand up and leave, when I remembered Asher's request.

So I stayed put in the chair and clicked out of the tabs I'd been using to research the deceased Mr. Mastronardi. Then I fished out my notebook from my bag, flipping to the page where I'd written Asher's information. I'd search that first and go from there.

The results were overwhelming.

From Wikipedia pages to government lists, the search results for this were about as opposite as could be from the small amount I'd been able to pull up on Frank. Deciding to start with the army lists, I found the order of battle for World War I on Wikipedia, which held links to separate pages for each division, regiment, and battalion.

Feeling like I was onto something, I scrolled down until I found the numbers matching Asher's division and regiment. My pulse quickened when I found it and clicked on the link.

The page pulled up, and I scanned through information about the regiment's motto and crest. I stopped at the seventh battalion after scrolling past the first few. The seventh had been the one Asher commanded. The first word under the heading was, "Unfortunately."

Swallowing my worries, I leaned in closer to the screen and read on. A metallic taste coated my tongue and my throat grew hot as I read:

"Unfortunately, this battalion developed a reputation of being untrustworthy in battle from the start of the war, with individual cases of cowardice. The unit commander was tried for dereliction of duty, and its soldiers reassigned to other units."

Heat rose up my neck, gathering in my face. I swallowed the taste of pennies in my mouth. Asher had been the unit commander they were talking about.

All I could think about was Asher telling me about his death. *Death in a war is valiant, something to be honored. I guess I'm not worried about why I'm still here because of that.*

Heck, maybe that *was* why he was still here. He'd mentioned how the worst thing someone could've called him was a coward. He'd gone on about how reputation was everything. That might be his unfinished business, his trauma.

I thought back to my history lessons and remembered the punishment for cowardice was often execution by firing squad. Was that how he died? My eyes began to water and I swiped away the moisture. Could I really tell Asher they had executed him for failing to fulfill his military duties?

My attention caught on the word *cowardice* as I noticed the word itself was a link. I clicked on it and a new page opened with another article. This one focused on the Shot at Dawn campaign.

I pored over the words on the screen, which detailed how the young men in World War I who had been shot for cowardice had most likely been suffering from shell shock or post-traumatic stress disorder. Their families have even been working to get them posthumously pardoned now that we were better educated on the subject of mental health.

My heart ached as I recalled Asher sharing about how scared he'd been to be in charge of the lives of so many young men.

I was almost halfway through the article when I felt someone standing behind me.

"Excuse me, Rosemary," Roger said in a quiet tone as he peered down at me.

I swear, give the man a cardigan, and he could step in for the children's television star, I thought as I blinked my dry eyes. I must've been reading too close to the screen.

"I didn't want to interrupt you—it looked like you were reading a very intense article—but we're closing." Roger inclined his head toward the clock on the wall.

Glancing around, the place had emptied since I'd last looked up.

"Oh, I'm so sorry." I closed out my screen and logged off the computer, shutting it down. I grabbed my notepad and scurried away. "Thank you."

"Any time," he said with a smile. "Have a great evening."

I tried to return the happy gesture, but the truth of it was, the weight of what I'd learned dragged at me like the anchor of a boat.

And even though I agreed with the more empathetic perspective I'd read about in that last article, I wondered if Asher would see it that way when he learned the truth about how he'd died.

17

As if I didn't have enough on my mind on the drive home, Mom called as my hatchback broke free of downtown and headed toward the beach. I thought about not answering, but she deserved better than that, better than a daughter who kept so much from her. And while I didn't want to tell her the ghostly, murdery parts of my current reality, I needed to at least be honest with her about the decision I'd made about Grandma's house.

"Hi, honey." Her voice had that honeyed ring to it when she tried to pretend she was okay but wasn't.

"Hey, Mom."

"How'd it go at the realtor's?"

My fingers tightened around the steering wheel. "Uh, well, not great. The only offer on the table was way under asking price, and so I turned it down. Gretta says I can get way more for the property and the business."

"Oh, that's interesting. That far under, huh?" She sounded shocked. "And you didn't come back with a different value? Maybe they undercut so you would compromise?"

"They might've done that," I conceded. "I don't know, Mom. It didn't feel right, someone trying to get a deal on Grandma's house."

Mom paused, and I realized right away I'd made a mistake. Grandma's house. That phrase and the inevitable emotion backing told Mom loud and clear that I liked it here, that I missed my grandmother and wished I'd reconciled with her before she died.

That sounds like a lot of information from two words, but this was my mom. She could tell my mood from a look, a sigh; even my silence gave her evidence. She knew me inside and out.

"Well, I'm sure the realtor will keep her eye out for other buyers," Mom said, her voice taut.

"Yes, she will," I lied. But honestly, I'd already upset her enough with that comment. I couldn't bear to break her heart by admitting that I might want to stay here, that I'd forgiven Grandma, even if she hadn't. I wished so intensely that Mom would read the diary and letter Grandma had left her. Maybe it would bring her closure like being here had for me.

"I love you, Mom," I said as I pulled up to the house. "I'll call you tomorrow."

"Are you sure you don't want me to come down there?" she asked after a beat.

"No," I said too quickly then puffed out my cheeks in frustration at how that sounded. "Uh—it's okay. It's probably for the better if you don't. I won't be much longer, I promise."

Great, there I went making promises again I wasn't sure I would keep. Just like I'd done with Asher.

"Okay. I won't come. I love you, Rosemary." Mom said the words in the quick way she always did when she told a lie and didn't want me to figure it out. She talked fast to cover up the tremor in her voice.

"Love you too, Mom." I hung up.

She wasn't lying about the loving me part, which meant she was contemplating coming here. My gut churned at the prospect of her showing up unannounced while I was having a conversation with my new ghost friend. Unfortunately, I didn't have time to wallow in that worry because I remembered my other, more pressing, worry: telling Asher about how he died.

Closing my eyes, I considered my options. Calling them options seemed cruel, honestly. I leaned my forehead on the steering wheel, but in all of my angst, I forgot the car was still in neutral, and I hadn't pulled the parking brake. So when I took my foot off the brake, the car lurched forward, and the front left side dipped down in an unsettling way.

Too late, I slammed my foot down to stop it. I jerked my head back and tried to ascertain what had happened.

The tea shop parking lot didn't have those concrete blockers to prevent cars from pulling too far forward. In my dilemma-filled distraction, I'd let the car roll off the pebbled parking area and onto the soft grass—or as it appeared from my dipping front end, into a hole in the grass.

I tried to reverse, but the tire just spun. Frustrated, I put the car back in neutral and got out. I'm not sure what I expected, but after trying to rock the car back and forth a little and push, I realized the motion was futile on my own. Either I needed to get Daphne and Carl to help—and I had no idea how helpful they would be in this kind of venture—or I would have to call a local tow truck to pull me out.

Grabbing my keys from the ignition, I stalked inside, my frustration and bad mood following me like a storm cloud.

Asher peered out the window looking out on the parking lot when I entered.

"I was about to come out and see what happened," he said, pointing to my car, teetering between the gravel and the grass. "So … what happened?" he added.

Just like that, I knew I couldn't tell him about the way he'd died. Not yet. Not until I'd looked into it more. Mom always said a good researcher verified their findings with at least three other sources. I'd run out of time to do so today. And before I told Asher, I had to make sure I'd gotten the correct information.

My mind frantically planned what I might say to him instead of the truth. First, I started with the easy part: answering his question about my car.

"I wasn't paying attention when I pulled in because I was talking to my mom on the phone, and I got my car stuck." I placed my hand on my sweaty forehead as I took in the sight of my vehicle.

He regarded me for a moment. "Do you want me to help?" he asked.

I pulled out my phone. "No, it's okay. If you got foggy after saving that mug yesterday, I'd hate to see what would happen if you tried to move my car. I'm sure there's at least one tow truck in this town. I'll just call them."

Asher cocked his head at me. "You seem agitated. Did you learn something about Frank?" I could tell he also meant, *or about me?* but wouldn't say it. "Or was it the talk with your mom?"

"Uh." I hooked my thumbs into my belt loops. "All of it?" I shuffled my feet on the carpet. "Sorry. It's been a weird day."

His gaze swept over my face. "Did you find anything on

me …?" he asked quietly, just when I thought he would stay silent.

"Asher, I'm so sorry. I …" I paused. "I … couldn't find what you're looking for." The lie tightened around my throat.

His eyes held so many questions. "Nothing?" was the only one he asked.

"There wasn't information on your specific group," I answered hastily, unsure why I didn't just tell him I needed more time. My cheeks flashed with heat. "The internet might have five million cat videos, but it didn't have any of the answers you want." I laughed.

Asher didn't join me. "Are you sure you searched in the correct places?" His tone was flat, but his face wasn't. A burning disappointment marred his features.

I considered adding that I could keep looking. But the thought of telling him even after I'd verified my sources now seemed unbearable.

Panicking, I said, "My mom used to be a research librarian for a university. I learned from the best."

"What about the local papers? Did you look through those?" he asked, the hope returning to his face.

I nodded, unable to even speak the lie. "Nothing," I added before tucking my chin in shame and studying my phone for a moment.

Asher threw his hands up. "Great, so I'm stuck here."

I scoffed, "Sorry you're stuck here I didn't realize it was so terrible."

Pacing, Asher let out a frustrated growl. "You don't understand. Are you sure you can't search again? If we find a better computer and bring it here, I can help you."

The image of Asher reading those terrible words over my shoulder made my awful shivers run down my spine.

"No," I blurted. "I'm sorry, but you're not going to find anything out there. Just let it go."

In my head, the last sentence sounded a lot more comforting, like a gentle urging. It came out much uglier, like an angry threat.

Asher, who'd been pacing again, whirled around to face me. He didn't have blood in his body—or have a body, for that matter—but I could've sworn his face reddened with outrage.

"You know what?" He spat out the words. "Don't bother calling about your car." He glanced behind him at the parking lot.

Before I knew what was happening, he disappeared through the wall. Running toward the door, I pulled it open in time to see Asher move his hands toward my car like he might push it back. A burst of energy whooshed off him so intensely the air pulsed in front of him. My car rolled backward.

I ran forward, flung open the door, and pulled the parking brake when it was free of the hole.

"Asher! Thank you," I said as I climbed out and shut the car door. "You didn't have—" I couldn't finish my thank you because Asher was already fading away.

"Bye, Rosie," he said, his words a distant whisper, his body a trace of its usual appearance.

And then, just like that, he disappeared, disintegrated like sugar dissolving in hot tea.

"Asher?" I yelled.

But he was gone.

18

I paced through the empty house hours later. Hunger gripped my stomach, but I didn't feel like making any food. I finished the rest of my pizza from my first day here, tears streaming down my face.

He was gone. Completely.

I realized there would be consequences for him using so much energy. That's why I'd told him I would call a tow truck. But I hadn't guessed the act would obliterate him. And then there was what he'd said to me, just before vanishing.

"Bye, Rosie."

He'd called me Rosie, which he hadn't ever done. But it was the *bye* that sent a chill down my spine. Matched with the hurt in his eyes, the way his face fell like he'd given up, that bye had seemed final.

I felt so stupid. In my wayward attempt to protect his feelings, I'd ended up hurting him worse than I imagined.

Would he even be back? I wondered.

He'd said he was foggy for an hour after moving that

book last week. He'd been the same way for a few hours after the mug incident. Those were both so much less intense than what he'd done with the car.

The house which had become so comforting, so warm and inviting since I'd come back, now felt too big, too quiet. Rain lashed at the picture windows in the tearoom, and so I retreated to the leather couch in the library with a mug of tea. I pulled a blanket around me and grabbed the book we'd been reading the other night, trying to lose myself in its pages, in the made-up world, in a world where I wasn't responsible for pushing away my friend.

I woke up Sunday morning with the headache that only comes after hours of crying. My nose was stuffed and runny, but other than that, I felt dehydrated.

Outside, the sky was still overcast and angry. The waves were more white than grayish blue, and I could see white-caps out as far as the first buoy, which meant the wind was blowing.

I scanned my surroundings for signs of Asher, expecting him to come back any moment. A part of me knew that even if he reappeared, he wouldn't come back here though. Not yet.

Within an hour of waking up, I decided I couldn't stay at the house all day or I would drive myself crazy. And while Chief Clemenson had given me reason to take the other teahouse owner, Jolene, off my list of suspects, I had yet to learn more about this yelling match Grandma and Doc Gallagher had gotten into the day she died. It was doubtful I'd be able to get anything out of the mayor in the middle of the day on a Monday, anyway, so this seemed like the best use of my time.

The retired doctor's address wasn't listed in the phone book or online, but I remember Althea mentioning he still lived downtown so I drove into Pebble Cove, hoping a local would tell me how to find the man. I parked in the same lot I'd been using all weekend and walked to the Marina Mug. Asher said that was where he learned the most town gossip. Either the patrons or Vicki might share information.

"Rosemary?" someone called as I rounded the corner to the café.

Turning around, Althea walked toward me, a cloth grocery bag hanging from one arm.

"Oh, hi." I smiled and stopped.

"You were sure on a mission," she said with a laugh. "You walked right past me."

I shook my head. "Sorry, I must've been focused. I was going to the Marina Mug."

"Sometimes you really need a coffee. I get it." She chuckled.

"Actually, I wanted to ask for some information." Gesturing toward her I said, "You might know."

She let her eyebrows rise, indicating she might.

"I'm looking for Doc Gallagher. Do you know where he lives?"

She pointed across the cove, a few doors down from the library. "He's in that blue house almost on the end of the beach."

"Thanks!" I said, and I almost left right then, in my excitement, but stopped myself, realizing I was being rude. "How are you?" I asked.

"I'm fine," she said, but she rubbed her chin. "Why are

you looking for Doc Gallagher?" she asked. "Is this because of the fights I told you about?"

I studied down at my hands for a moment but then nodded. I wasn't ready to admit to her I thought my grandma had been murdered, though, so I said, "I'm trying to learn about her life and that includes the good and the bad." I shrugged as if it weren't a big deal, as if this weren't life and death.

Althea studied me for a long time like she might be worried about my mental health, but she must've decided I was okay because she said, "Well, good luck, dear."

I waved to her and headed down the street, toward the retired doctor's house.

The sun peeked through the clouds, but they still spit rain, so the light offered only a minuscule amount of relief from the cold. I pulled my jacket tighter as I knocked on the door of the blue house at the end of the cove.

"Coming," said an man from within.

All too late, I realized that if this man was a suspect in my grandma's murder, I probably shouldn't be going inside his house alone. It was cold outside but not unbearably so. I tried to make a plan of how to avoid entering if he invited me inside.

In that moment, I wished I'd thought this through better, that I'd thought to bring Althea along with me. Even more, I wished Asher were here with me.

The man who opened the front door a few moments later struck me as about ten years younger than Carl. But unlike my neighbor's stooped and angry demeanor, this man stood tall and wore a broad smile. He wasn't much taller than me, but there was an air about him that told me he had no problem commanding the respect of a room.

"Hello," he said, keeping his grin in place. Any cheerfulness faded though. "Wait, you look too much like …" He trailed off, rubbing a hand across the gray stubble on his jaw.

I curled my toes inside my shoes to release my nervous energy. "I'm Helen Woodmere's granddaughter, Rosemary." I held out my hand to shake his, unsure if he would even want to after the disappointed way his face fell when he realized who I was.

Behind him, I noticed a woman peek around the corner. The doctor pulled the door closer to him so I couldn't see inside.

"Right. I heard you were in town." He took my hand and shook it, squeezing tight for a moment before letting go.

His hands were quintessential doctor's hands: cold and smooth, probably from washing them so often. He didn't invite me in but leaned against the frame of the open door.

"I'm really sorry about your grandmother's passing." He smoothed his graying hair flat with one of those cold hands.

"Why are you sorry?" I asked, knowing it was a cheap shot, but needing to broach the subject before he closed the door in my face.

His eye twitched. "It's just—it's what people say." His cheeks reddened, and he looked away from me.

"Is it?" I asked, venting all my frustration from my day of missing Asher toward this doctor. "Or do you feel guilty about the huge fight you got into with her the day she died?" I asked, stopping short of accusing him of murder.

The doctor's face fell. "You heard about that?" he asked.

"Heard it happened but not what it was about. Care to enlighten me about that?" I clamped my mouth shut after that last question.

I'd done a lot more talking than I probably should've already and was ready to fall back to my old standard—listening. But while I expected him to open up like everyone else in town had with me so far, this man made it clear he was a closed book.

Crossing his arms, he glared at me. "It wasn't about anything. It was none of your business, and I need to go." He growled out the demand.

Before I could say anything more, he slammed the door shut in my face.

I stood there stunned and frozen for a second before anger welled up inside me and thawed me out. That wasn't the behavior of an innocent person. Turning on my heel, I stomped away from the doctor's house. Loneliness wrapped up around me, and I wished Asher were here so I could talk through this. I even searched for Meow in town as I walked, knowing his company wouldn't be the same as having Asher, but it would be something.

As I walked past Wallace's grocery store, I popped inside to grab a sandwich. Having food in my stomach gave me a much-needed burst of hope. Inside that hopeful state, the possibility that Asher might have reappeared consumed me, and I drove home probably a little too fast in my excitement.

But there was still no Asher. Not inside. Not out on the beach.

It wasn't until my second pass through the house I got an idea.

Asher had mentioned how he'd spent a lot of time in the abandoned cannery with other local ghosts lately. The hurt on his face in the moments before he vanished made me positive he wouldn't come back here anytime soon. If that were the case, it would be worth it to check and see if he was at the cannery.

Carl waved as I drove down the easement, but I only returned the wave, too excited about my idea to stop and talk. It was only after I turned onto Misty Drive that I realized I didn't know how to get to the cannery. Seeing there were no cars coming behind me on the road, I slowed my car and contemplated going back and asking Carl for directions. But as I rolled forward, I saw a turn off ahead. The road was pitted and potholed. I took it, hoping that its forgotten state meant I'd chosen the correct road.

Desperation Cliff loomed ahead of me confirming the road was right, and I started climbing up. I pulled the car to a slow stop for a moment on the top of the cliff, rolling down my window and letting the whoosh of sea air push past me. Even from the safety of my car, I imagined the teetering fear of being balanced on top of the cliff and how scary peering down at the rocks hundreds of feet below might be.

Rolling up my window with a shiver, I pressed on the accelerator and proceeded down the hill. The large concrete building at the bottom of the hill was almost as foreboding as the cliff, and I realized my day wasn't about to get any more pleasant. I longed to curl up in the teahouse's library with a blanket, a book, and a cup of tea. But Asher might be in here.

If he was, I had to find him, had to bring him back.

Parking in the cracked, weed-infested lot in front of the old building, I steeled my courage. There was a long list of reasons why I shouldn't enter. On that list were things like how this place looked straight out of a horror movie, not to be outdone by the disturbing fact that no one knew I was here. But curiosity and a burning need to find Asher pushed me forward.

The broken windows looked like missing teeth on a

grimacing concrete face, and I got out of my car before I changed my mind. Even though the main doors had been boarded up and chained shut, one of the large windows to the right had been completely kicked in, and I stepped through to enter the shell of a building.

Inside smelled of decaying fish and stale air. Other than a few metal tables and old broken machines, the cannery was empty. An inch or two of dirt and dust collected on the floor, and my shoes left prints as I walked forward. Luckily, I didn't see any other footprints; I really didn't want to think about the kinds of humans who might hang out in a place like this. Of course, all I cared about was the nonliving, someone who wouldn't make footprints.

"Asher?" I called, my voice mixed with the ocean waves echoing off the bare concrete walls.

And even though I recognized it was only the sound of my voice, it was comforting. So I kept talking.

"Asher, I don't know if you're here, or if you'll respond to me, even if you are. I'm so sorry about hurting your feelings." I talked as I walked up to a small office. The door hung on its hinges, leaning against the inside wall.

Inside the office, ancient floral wallpaper peeled like birch tree bark. Reaching out, I tried to flatten the curls with my fingers only to have them spring back and crackle at me in protest. A long-forgotten desk sat in one corner. I turned around. Asher wasn't in here.

Moving back into the large main room, I kept talking.

"I met with Doc Gallagher today, and he's hiding something. I can feel it. I know we thought the mayor was our best suspect, but I think this fight Grandma had with the retired doctor the day she died is important. The way he got so angry, slammed the door in my face, I think he could be the person who killed her." I swallowed, shaking my head to keep frustrated tears at bay. I meandered over to a window overlooking the beach below. The breeze kicking up from the waves felt like a lifeline as it filled my lungs, allowed me to breathe again.

Fresh as the air by the window was, those loud, crashing waves made it so I didn't hear the sounds behind me at first.

19

A voice that wasn't mine broke through the wind and the waves.

"Psh. The doc? Doubtful."

I spun around, heart racing with excitement.

"Ash—?" His name died on my lips as I took in the two men entering the room. Both were older: neither were Asher.

They walked shoulder to shoulder.

"Excuse me," I said, inching forward. "Why would you say that? Why is what I said doubtful?"

It was then I realized their feet weren't making any prints in the dusty ground as they crossed the room. Afternoon sun shone through the broken windows, shining through their transparent bodies. My chest constricted in fear for a moment. Asher had said other ghosts hung out here. I should've expected this.

The surprised expressions on their faces as they spun to watch me approach abated some of that fear.

"What did you say?" the older of the two asked, his forehead furrowing as his gaze flicked over me in surprise. "You can see us?"

Both men had graying hair—though one had much more than the other. They wore similar denim jackets with collars lined in a white sheared material and worn jeans. Unlike Asher, the men appeared contemporary, at least from the current century.

Squaring my shoulders, I held eye contact with the one who'd asked the questions and said, "Yes, I can see you, and I can hear you too. What did you mean a moment ago when you said *doubtful*?"

The man open and closed his mouth in surprise before finally answering. "Uh—well, that thing you said about the doc." He ran a hand over the back of his ghostly neck. "There's no way the doc killed anyone, let alone a grandma. Who is she, by the way? Your grandma?"

"Helen Woodmere."

The men shared a glance and laughed. "Yeah," the older one said through a chuckle. "No way Doc Gallagher did anything to hurt her."

I put a hand on my hip in disbelief. "And how can you be so sure?"

"They loved each other," the younger man said.

I coughed. "He has to be at least twenty years younger than her." As I said it, I realized how stodgy and old fashioned I sounded. I mean, there were couples with larger age differences who made things work.

The older man sniffed. "Nah, not romantically, I don't think. There was like a respect between them. They went to each other when they had problems. Disagreed on just about every topic but loved to debate."

As I listened, doubt surrounded me like stars around a cartoon character after they've run straight into a brick wall.

I blinked in an effort to get rid of them. "How do you know that?" I asked.

Then I remembered how I knew a lot of things that I couldn't explain because of Asher and Meow. These men were ghosts too. They probably had access to way more information than I realized.

The older ghost frowned. "They used to fight all the time in the tea shop, in the café, in the doctor's office. Heck, those two fought anywhere they could. But mostly, I know about their true feelings because of Lois."

"Lois?" I asked.

The younger one nodded. "Yeah, if you want to know about every detail, you've got to talk to Lois for sure."

"And she is?"

"The woman who used to live in his house. Still hangs out there," the younger one said.

"Probably more than she should," the older man said, widening his eyes.

The younger one cringed. "Yeah, I'd say she's got a bit of a crush on the good doctor. A little unhealthy, if you ask me. She shouldn't be hanging around a living man searching for love."

"You only say that because you want her to come hang around you more," the older man said, jabbing his elbow toward the younger one.

Drowning out their friendly banter, my mind flashed back to the doctor's house, to the woman I caught peeking around the corner behind him. I'd assumed she lived there, that she was his wife.

"Healthy or not, she hears everything that goes on in that house. She'd know for sure." The older man dipped his chin.

"Okay. I'll talk to Lois. Thanks." I moved my shoe in an

arch in front of me, leaving a half-moon mark in the dust and dirt. "You two haven't—er—seen anyone else around here lately, have you?"

"Who?" The old man cocked his head.

"Asher Benson."

"That twenties kid?" he asked.

Unsure if he was talking about how Asher appeared to be in his twenties or if he was from the nineteen twenties, I just nodded. Even though I knew Asher technically died sometime in 1918, I figured it was close enough.

"We haven't seen him for a few days. Been showing up a lot lately, but didn't show up at all this weekend." The younger man spoke, but they both considered me, as if realizing at the same moment that I was the reason for Asher's absence.

"Okay," I said, downcast. "If you do, would you tell him I'm looking for him? Rosemary," I added, pointing to my chest.

"Max." The younger one held out a hand toward me, before pulling it back sheepishly. "Sorry, I still forget."

"Tim." The old man lifted his chin in a way that was either a greeting or he was sizing me up. I chose to believe the former.

"Nice to meet you." I was about to leave when my feet froze, and I turned back toward the men. "Are you both okay?" My cheeks heated. "I mean, you're here because you have unfinished business. Do you need any help?"

Max's face softened. "That's very kind of you, Miss Rosemary. I'm good. Took me until a year or two back to figure out that my wife offed me. I've got all the closure I'll ever get in that department."

"And I don't want to cross over because my mother-in-law is on the other side, and I can't stand the idea of having to see her again," Tim said with a rough laugh.

I frowned. "So you're both here even though you don't have to be?" I asked.

Max said, "Oh, I've got unfinished business all right. Haunting my ex-wife is a full-time job."

"Haunting her? Shouldn't she go to jail? Maybe you're still around because you haven't gotten the justice you deserve."

Max glanced at Tim and laughed again. "Believe me, Rosemary, the ways I've been able to make her life miserable is better than any sentence she could ever receive in a jail."

My stomach flipped. Here I'd thought these two men were nice; they'd been growing on me. Now I wasn't so sure.

Tim got the real meaning behind my question. "But yes, we can stay here if we chose to. Some souls don't care to move on."

I thought of Meow. Apparently, cats weren't the only slippery souls out there.

"Helps when you've got a friend by your side," Max said, smiling over at Tim.

The gesture made my heart ache thinking of Asher, my mom, my grandmother. Aware that my pain was probably written on my face, I scratched at my nose to cover.

"Okay, just checking. Good day, gentlemen." I gave the men a quick salute and then jogged back toward the parking lot, eager to put this place in my rearview mirror.

The sun was dipping down close to the horizon and I groaned. I really didn't want to go home to an empty house again. When I pulled the car toward the end of the abandoned road that led to the cannery, I noticed Misty Road continued to the left. It curved upward toward the tree-filled hills sitting behind Pebble Cove.

Up on one hill, I saw warm lights blinking through the dark greens and browns. A large white building sat tucked up there. I thought about Althea telling me about her restorative center: quiet, secluded, right outside of town.

That must be it, I realized. And without Asher around to talk with, her offer to come visit sounded better than ever. Max and Tim had reminded me how much better life could be with someone to listen. Althea had been my grandma's best friend. She felt like the right person to talk to about my suspicions.

So instead of turning right to go back to the teahouse, I took a left and followed the winding road up into the forest. About a mile in, a hand-carved sign told me to turn left for The Pines.

The place was breathtaking. A huge white farmhouse sat on top of a grassy knoll on an acre-sized clearing in the trees. Also in the clearing were two large garden plots, a chicken coop, a winding circular labyrinth, and a barn. Yellow lights glowed from every window and twinkled from small decorative lamps along the pathway leading up to the house.

Almost all the parking spaces were full, but I found one closer to the barn. When I stepped out of my car, the echoed sounds of birds chirping in the trees made me close my eyes, and I tipped my head back. The crashing waves of the beach were a quiet white noise in the background. Other than that, the place was silent.

I squared my shoulders, already feeling better.

Althea greeted me as I walked up to the house. She wore a blue apron and an inviting smile.

"I'm so glad you joined us." She wiped her hands on the apron and then held them out as she met me halfway on the stairs and pulled me into a hug.

I squeezed her tight, reveling in the feeling of a hug after such a bad day. "It's gorgeous up here."

I turned away from the house to survey the property. From my new vantage point on the stairs, I could see the ocean over the tops of the evergreens.

"My bedroom has the best view," Althea said, pointing up at a small window under the peak of the roof in the attic. "It's the one room I'll never rent out."

I looked back at her. Her rosy cheeks just about glowed in the light from the house.

"You have quite the full house here," I said as I motioned to the parking lot. "I can see why. It's the most peaceful place I've set foot in a long time."

Althea beamed. "Thank you, Rosemary. That means a lot. Yes, we've almost got a full house. Just one room open at the moment."

I swallowed, realizing that room had probably been reserved for the dead man who'd washed up on my beach.

Althea seemed to realize the same thing because she tugged at her shirt and said, "Anyway, come in. The guests finished with dinner already, but there's still plenty to eat if you're hungry." She ushered me up the porch steps.

"I'm actually starving," I said. My day had been emotionally and physically draining.

She held the door open for me, and a wonderful combination of garlic, butter, onions, and roasting veggies swirled out from inside.

"Everyone's up in their rooms already for their nightly meditation time," Althea explained as we walked into a quiet dining room with a large table with service for at least ten people. The table was cleared of any signs of dinner, each chair pushed in and ready for the next meal. "But we can go into the kitchen to chat." She pointed to a set of swinging double doors at the back of the room.

Pushing through them, she led me into a huge commercial kitchen with stainless steel workspaces and racks.

"This is where that delicious smell is coming from," I said, closing my eyes as I pulled in a greedy nose-full of the scents swirling around the kitchen. The good smells lingered even though dinner had been cleaned up and put away from the looks of the clean countertops. "Do you do all the cooking yourself?" I asked, shaking my head in disbelief as I considered the amazing workspace.

"Oh, no." Althea laughed and walked over to a stainless steel refrigerator. She pulled open the double doors. "I have a wonderful cook, but she only works lunch and dinner prep. She leaves right after dinner's ready, so I serve and clean up."

From inside the fridge, Althea pulled a glass container full of the roasted veggies I'd smelled upon entering the place. On top of it, she stacked a smaller container that held a few cups of fluffy quinoa. Then she tucked a bottle in the crook of her elbow, grabbed a large uncovered bowl of greens with her free hand, and used her shoulder to push the doors closed behind her.

"Tonight we had a quinoa and roasted veggie salad with our famous citrus avocado dressing. Does that sound okay?" she asked, depositing the containers onto one of the shiny, clean surfaces.

"It sounds amazing," I said, mouth watering in anticipation.

Althea gestured to a barstool across the counter from her. "Sit. We can chat while I get this ready for you."

I took a seat, resting my elbows on the cool steel. I followed her movements as she prepared a plate for me. "I can't thank you enough, Althea," I said after a moment. "I really needed this. It was a hard day." My gaze fell to my hands for a quick second.

Althea paused. Her face crinkled in concern. "I was missing her a lot today too," she said, assuming I was talking about my grandma and not the fact that I'd scared away my ghostly friend.

I nodded because it was easier than explaining the truth.

"You're sticking around, then?" she asked, pausing in the middle of filling a plate with vibrant green lettuce.

"I don't know." I chewed on my lip. "I'm torn. I think my mom would love for me to sell the place and never look back. She wants me to live down the road and work in the same building as her forever so she can monitor me."

I cringed at the way I'd worded that. It made my mom come off badly.

But Althea only grinned as she put some quinoa and roasted veggies into a bowl and then stuck them into the microwave. "I'm sure she does. She almost lost you, twice. That's enough to drive most mothers to their breaking point. I'd love to meet her. She sounds like an amazing woman."

"She is." I exhaled my relief. "And I get that she worries about me, but I also know that she sacrificed so much for me … still does. I want her to live her own life now that I'm an adult."

The microwave beeped, and Althea grabbed the steaming dish from inside. "Oh, honey, being a mother never ever stops. But it's very sweet of you to think of her like that. I would say the most pressing question is, what do you want?"

Without thinking, I said, "I want to live here." Eyelids snapping open in my surprise, I glanced up at Althea. She was grinning from ear to ear. "I love my grandma's house," I continued.

"Your house," Althea said, pointing a spoon at me as she arranged the warm veggies onto the bed of lettuce.

"Right. My house. I love the house. I think I'd like to reopen the tea shop too. I don't know if I'll be as good at the tea thing as my grandma, but—" I stopped myself before I said *Asher can always help me*, like I wanted to. "I can always learn," I said instead.

Althea popped a wayward piece of squash into her mouth. "That's the attitude. Well, I'd love to have you stick around. You know, your grandma sold her teas to me too. We had a bit of a partnership going. I'd love to continue that if you're going to run the place." She drizzled some dressing over the plate and then pushed in toward me.

I grabbed the fork she handed over and speared my first bite. It was divine.

"Almost everything was grown right here on the property," Althea said, reading my expression.

"It's amazing."

It took me much less time than it probably should have to finish that salad. While I ate, Althea cleaned up, returning the containers to the fridge and pouring us each a glass of water.

Once my plate was empty, Althea cocked her head to one side. "Okay, Rosemary. Are you ready to tell me the *real* reason you're here?"

20

Gulping down the last chewed mouthful of salad, I asked. "Am I that obvious?"

Althea took my plate and put it in the large farmhouse sink behind her. "Your grandma had the same tell," she said, gesturing to my fingers tapping on the tabletop. "She could never keep her fingers still when she had more on her mind than she was letting on."

I took a sip of my water before looking Althea in the eyes and saying, "I think she was murdered."

Althea's lips parted. "What?" She gasped out the word.

I grimaced, not wanting to hurt the woman who'd been so kind to me. "I'm sorry to spring it on you like that. It's just some things don't add up; they don't seem right. She didn't die of a heart attack like everyone assumed."

Althea placed a hand on the counter to steady herself. "And what made you think this?" she asked quietly.

Cursing the fact I couldn't tell her I'd gotten my information from a ghost, I considered my options.

"I mean, did she seem like she was that sick?" I asked,

propping my elbows on the stainless steel countertop. "The last time you saw her?"

Althea pulled in a deep breath. "No, now that you mention it. I saw her that morning. She came here with a tea delivery. She looked great, actually." Althea drummed her fingers on the counter. "But heart conditions can turn at the drop of a pin."

I frowned, remembering how Asher had told me about Althea's past as a doctor. "And she's already been cremated, so we can't figure out if that was the case or not."

"Sorry, dear," Althea said. "It was in her will. We didn't have any reason to act otherwise … at the time."

I put up a hand. "It's not your fault. There are a few people who had these huge issues with her. I can't help but wonder if they could've gotten mad enough to try to get her out of the way."

"Like Sam Hoff, you mean?" Althea's expression clouded over.

My gaze flicked from her face to her grim-set mouth. "Yes, you agree?"

"That slimeball has been wishing your grandmother would shut up for years, but the fact that she died right before his special election, just in time for him to undermine the lead she was gaining against him, does sound especially suspicious." Althea pulled a stool toward her and sat on it. "That means I was right about what I overheard …" she scoffed.

"What did you overhear?" I asked, leaning in close.

Althea's eyes widened. "Last year, Sam hired a consultation company to run a report about the financial boost the outlet mall would give our city. At the time, Meow was still mayor, and Sam's group was trying to sway members of the council. The consultants stayed here during their visit. I overheard them discussing numbers, saying the locals would likely lose money on the outlets, but I couldn't be sure they were talking about our town."

"What? Why didn't you tell people?" I stood as if I might drive down to Pebble Cove right now to tell them.

Althea raised a hand to calm me. "I didn't have any actual proof. I only think I heard them discussing it." She slouched at the admission. "And I'm not exactly well trusted around here, or anywhere, anymore." Her gaze flitted over to a shelf where a single book rested.

The title was *I'm Okay, Really*. The cover featured a teenage girl.

"Why's that?" I asked tentatively. Asher had mentioned she'd quit medicine.

Althea sighed. "I used to be a doctor. Did you know that?"

Having no way to explain how I would, I shook my head.

"About ten years ago, I misdiagnosed a young girl." Althea nodded toward the book. "Her parents kept coming in, telling me something was wrong. One week it was meningitis, the next it was mono, then the next it was multiple sclerosis. She didn't show the right symptoms for any of it, so I became sure one or both of them had Munchausens." Althea rested her head in her hands for a moment. "It turns out, she had a late-onset case of a very rare disease caused by an enzyme deficiency."

"All doctors make mistakes sometimes," I said, unwilling to believe there had been such fallout from one mistake.

"Yes, but not all our patients get book deals and a line of television appearances after the truth comes out. I'd talked with her privately once about how I worried her parents might be creating an illness that wasn't there. I recognized it was wrong, that I shouldn't talk to a minor like that, but I was really worried for the girl's safety at that point, before we found out what it really was. That was my biggest mistake. She sued me for emotional damages, told everyone how I'd made her doubt her own parents."

I leaned forward, taking Althea's hand in mine. "I'm so sorry."

"I left the practice, knowing I would never be taken seriously again. And I ran here. I still like to help people feel better; I just do it holistically now." She gestured to the surrounding house. "But I keep her there." She pointed to the book. "That reminds me I have to keep professional boundaries with the people I treat here. It reminds me I'm not always right. And as welcoming as the people of Pebble Cove have been, they don't hesitate to remind me of my mistake if I ever question *the way they do things around here*." She let out a long exhale. "If I questioned Sam Hoff, Pebble Cove's golden boy, he would throw that mistake back in my face and convince people not to believe me. Plus when he shared the report, it showed the outlets would be profitable, so I doubted what I heard. But Sam seemed to know the consultants. He could've paid them to put out a false report."

Folding my arms in front of my chest, I said, "I wouldn't put it past him. But if he knows it's a bad investment, having a secret stake in the development wouldn't help him. Why would he still push for it?"

Althea's nostrils flared. "Secret stake in the development?"

"I was in the wrong place at the wrong time—well, maybe right time—and saw evidence that he is behind the development company that's pitching the outlets."

"Even though he swore he wouldn't get involved since it would be ethically wrong." Althea's eyes narrowed.

"Yep. But if he had the study done, why would he go ahead with this if he knows it's not going to be profitable?"

Her face lit up in recognition. "When I overheard the consultants, they mentioned the only ones who would get rich would be the developers."

"So he's willing to hurt the town and the townspeople to line his pockets." I balled my fingers into a fist.

Althea brought a hand up to her mouth. "And your grandmother was in his way. Rosemary, you might be right. How do we prove this?"

I wet my lips. "I'm working on it. I need to get into the town hall, though. There might be more in there that we could use as evidence."

Determination leaked from her features. "I don't have any way to help you with that."

"It's okay. I might have an in." I stood. "In the meantime, if you can find any evidence of where he was the night my grandma died, that would be helpful."

Althea said she would do her best.

"We need to prove he was by her house just before sunset," I added. "That's when he switched her medication."

"Got it," she said, but her face screwed up in confusion for a moment. "Wait, you said a few people were suspicious. Who else are you looking into?"

I dipped my head to one side. "Well, I suspected her neighbor, Carl, for a bit."

Althea widened her eyes. "Oh, they hated each other for sure."

I waved a hand to dismiss her thoughts. "He didn't do it though. The man's grumpy but harmless."

Althea exhaled what sounded like a pent-up breath. "That's good. I'd hate to think of you right next door to that man if he could've hurt Helen."

"I suspected Jolene, the other tea shop owner, for a while, but I discovered she's been in a cast for a few weeks now."

"Yes," Althea said. "The poor woman slipped by the marina during a late frost. It was like a perfect storm of bad luck. She lost her footing at just the wrong place when no one else was around to help, hit one of the big rocks down in the marina in just the wrong spot, and broke her leg in two places. We've been bringing her meals since she can hardly get around her house."

I tugged at the hem of my shirt. "And the last one I'm looking into is Doc Gallagher." Althea opened her mouth as if to combat my claim. I held a hand up to stop her. "I understand now that they had a weird love slash hate thing going, but I have a few more things I want to ask before I scratch him from my list."

"Need help?" Althea asked.

Thinking of the ghosts telling me to visit Lois, I wrinkled my nose. "No, I'm okay. This is one person I need to question myself." I took a step back toward the door. "But thank you so much for your kindness tonight, for listening, and feeding me."

She grinned, following me. "You're welcome any time, Rosemary. I mean it." She reached out and took my hands in hers. "I miss Helen so much, but having you around is almost like having a piece of her back."

The warmth expanding through my heart ever since I walked into this house burst and filled my whole body.

"I feel the same way around you," I said, squeezing her hand before letting it go.

"I'll let you know if I can dig up anything about Sam's alibi or lack thereof." She led me to the front door.

I gripped the handle. It had to be Sam. Suspicion surrounded the man. Heck, he was steeping in it. Althea hugged me goodbye, and I followed the lights down the pathway, feeling full and happy for the first time since Asher disappeared.

On the drive home, I called my mom.

"Hey, honey." Her familiar voice didn't just fill the car because she was on speakerphone, but also my heart because she was exactly who I needed to talk to.

"Hi, Mom." I smiled. "There's something I need to tell you."

"Sure. What's up?" Silence filled the space after her question.

Althea had been right. Mom loved me and wanted what was best for me. I needed to be honest with her. She would understand; she would be happy for me. I exhaled as I turned onto Misty Drive.

"I want to stay." I didn't blurt out the words but said them in a slow and measured way, so she would understand that I was serious.

There was a long pause. "I was worried about this." She sighed. "Honey, I don't think that's the right decision."

"Wait, why? Mom, I know you want me to stay close, but I'm twenty-five, I need to live my life … we both do." I cringed at how harsh that sounded.

"Rosemary, what's the real reason you turned down the first offer?" she asked but then didn't even give me time to answer. "Did the locals talk you out of it? I know he was there to develop, but he swore Helen's house wouldn't be part of that. He wanted to live nearby during the development and construction of a different job."

I pulled into the teahouse parking lot and stopped, my foot stomping down on the brake so hard that the car and my body swayed forward. But it was nothing compared to the lurch that happened in my heart and lungs.

"Mom, what did you say?" My question came out a shaky whisper.

"Okay, so I may have talked to the guy who made the offer on the house. He came by the library and was chatting with Sally about his upcoming trip to Pebble Cove, how he might be looking to move there. I simply nudged him toward Helen's house."

A cold sweat crept down my neck. "What was his name?"

"Frank, of course. Didn't the realtor tell you that when she explained his offer?"

"Mom, this isn't good. You knew Frank Mastronardi?" My voice rose along with my heartbeat.

"Honey, calm down. What's the problem?"

"Mom," I said, cutting her off. "Frank is dead. His body washed up on the beach the day I got here."

The gasp she gave sent a chill down my spine.

21

Once Mom had replenished the air in her lungs, she used it to tell me exactly what I didn't want to hear.

"Rosemary, you need to get out of that town right now. If not, I'm coming to get you."

Even though I'd just turned off my car, the cold, not-quite-spring air already seeped in through the windows. The waves rolled in the distance, almost giving the illusion I wasn't alone in this conversation with my mother.

"Mom." I closed my eyes. "I'm okay, really. Frank Mastronardi killed himself. He jumped off a cliff near Grandma's house and washed up on her beach. No one killed him. Well, the police chief might think I did, but now you can call him and explain why he had my name written in his date book."

But as much as my words made sense to me, Mom was having none of it. "I'm serious, Rosemary Marie Woodmere. I don't want you staying there. That man wanted to invest. Why would he kill himself?"

Unsure how to answer that, I said, "I don't know, Mom.

But my friend and I are getting to the bottom of it. Don't worry. Please."

Mom sucked in an audible breath on the other end of the line. "Friend?" she asked softly.

I smiled, thinking of Asher. "Yes, Mom. I have a friend." Althea and Meow came to mind. "A few friends, actually. I fit in here, feel settled for the first time in a long time." I swallowed as my voice quaked. I didn't want her to think I had a bad childhood or that I didn't appreciate everything she'd done for me, all the sacrifices she'd made. "I miss you, so much, but this feels right."

"So you're serious about staying?" Her question wasn't angry or accusatory. Actually, that's what made it so heartbreaking.

If she'd yelled and ordered me to come home again, I don't think it would've hurt so much. But the quiet acceptance to her tone sounded like a sad rejection.

"I am, Mom." I kept my words quiet. "I'm learning a lot about Grandma, and"—I took a fortifying breath—"we all made mistakes. She loved us so much. She was wrong, sure, but I wish I'd come and made up with her before she died." Tears burned at the edges of my eyes. "It might be helpful for you to read the diary she left you and the letter. She gave them to you for a reason."

A silence sat on the other end, turning my stomach in knots. Finally, Mom said, "I'll think about it. I've got to close up the library. We'll talk tomorrow."

My heart ached. She'd shut down, like she did for a while after Dad died. "Okay," I said, doing the only thing I knew how: be there when she was ready to open back up. "I love you, Mom."

"Love you too, honey." Her end of the line clicked off, and my phone dropped the call.

Darkness surrounded the car, and I ran inside, turning on all the lights I could. Somehow having lights on made it feel like I wasn't alone. And even though I'd just convinced my mom I was okay, that I had friends, that things were going well here, my empty house made me realize all too quickly that things had changed.

"Asher, where are you?" I asked the empty library as I pulled a blanket around my shoulders. "Please, come back."

My eyelids slid closed, but I didn't fight sleep. Tomorrow I needed to get some information from a ghost, and even though it wasn't the ghost I really wanted to see, I hoped she would bring me one step closer to the truth.

"Does this guy ever leave his house?" I whispered to Meow the next day as I surveyed Doc Gallagher's blue house from the boardwalk.

Meow lay on his side in the middle of the sidewalk, blinking in the sun. While it had poured this morning, the rain had let up as I came into town. For the last half an hour, passersby had stepped on his splayed body, but their feet washed right through him. He seemed offended at first, swishing his tail in quick, agitated jerks, but not enough to get up and move out of the sun. Just like Asher, I was sure his love of sunbeams was more a habit or a memory than a feeling.

At the moment, we were alone, and I needed to talk through my plan. Unfortunately, I didn't have a plan at all if Doc Gallagher never left his place. From the large sliding glass doors and picture windows facing the water, I could see him making coffee and reading the newspaper. Lois shadowed him during every activity. Those ghosts yesterday at the cannery weren't kidding; Lois acted as if she and the retired doctor were married.

After forty-seven minutes, I placed my hands on my knees and stood. "Okay, Meow. I'm going in."

The cat watched me with emerald eyes and then trotted after me as I made my way down to the doctor's house. If the man wouldn't leave, I was going to have to figure out some way to get Lois to come outside to me. I pursed my lips. This would be a heck of a lot easier if he didn't already know who I was. He was less than eager to invite me inside yesterday, and that had been before I'd made him mad.

But even though the cannery ghosts had assured me he wouldn't hurt my grandma, there was something there. What had they fought about the day she died?

Steeling myself with courage and straightening up to my full height, I poked at the doorbell next to the front door of Doc Gallagher's house. Today there was no friendly call from inside. The door swung open to reveal a peeved-looking retiree.

"You just can't leave it alone, can you?" he grumbled, sneering at me through the gap in the door. "And now you're sitting outside my house watching me?" He gestured to the bench I'd occupied until a few moments ago.

Cringing, I said, "You saw me there?"

He rolled his eyes. "You were only short a pair of binoculars, and you would've been a genuine stalker." A sigh heaved his fishermen's-wool-sweater-covered chest up and down. "What do you want, Miss Woodmere?"

My mind raced with ideas of how to get Lois to come out and talk to me. Short of yelling her name and running away, I didn't have much. Remembering the sticky notes all over Grandma's house, I got an idea that might work.

"Well, as you know, my grandmother died." *Hey, it*

couldn't hurt to remind him of my recent loss. "And I've been going through her belongings, but she left a note ..." I widened my eyes as my brain latched on to an idea. "And I can't figure out what the note means. So I wondered if you could help me figure that out." I waited for his reaction.

The doctor's face paled like he might be sick. "A note? Why do you think I would be able to help? Is is about me?" He asked the three questions in such quick succession that it reminded me of my mom whenever she had a difficult time with a situation.

My face heated at his odd reaction. It looked like I'd been right not to discount him as a suspect. The man was hiding something.

A little smug about flustering him, I leaned in close, narrowing my eyes. "It is." But my cockiness quickly dissipated as I realized I had no idea what this nonexistent note might've said about him.

Just then, I saw Lois flit behind him, across the hall, visible through the open door.

"Uh—the note said, 'Lois, I know you're in there! I need to talk to you. It's very important. Please come outside and meet me, Lois!'" I projected my voice into the house in hope she would hear me. Waves of heat rose in my cheeks as I took in Doc Gallagher's confused expression. "Weird, huh?"

Please don't ask how that has anything to do with you, I pleaded, not having thought through my plan that far. At the same time, I listened, hoping for a response from Lois.

"How does that note have anything to do with me?" he asked, his upper lip curling.

I almost groaned.

Pressing my lips together for a moment, I said, "Your address was on the note." I gave him an I-don't-know-either shrug. I craned my neck to see inside, around him, but he stepped in my way, closing the door even more.

He clenched his teeth in frustration. "That's because Lois Butler used to live in this house before I bought it," he said, biting out the information like he recognized it was the only way to get rid of me. "She and your grandmother were friends back in the day. That's probably all it was. It must've been an old note." He raised an eyebrow as if asking if that was all.

I was about to slump my shoulders and slink away in defeat when I heard someone yell out from inside, "Were not! We were not friends! I hated Helen."

Eyes widening at the surprising outburst, I took one last stab, throwing any remaining hope of coming out of this looking sane out the window.

"Okay, well, thank you, Doctor Gallagher, for your time and information. And as my grandma said in her note, 'Lois! Come outside, please! We need to talk!'" I paused, hoping she'd heard my plea.

The doctor's features creased in a way that, had he still been practicing medicine, would've made me worried he might have me committed to a psychiatric ward.

"So weird, right?" I said before jogging away from his house. I swear Meow shook his head at me as we left. "What? It's not like you had a better plan," I told the cat.

He licked a paw and flicked his tail.

"I'm fully aware that she won't come out now and what I pulled was crazy. But she wasn't coming out in the first place, so we're in the same spot we were before."

And just as I turned to leave, I walked right through a middle-aged woman.

"Bah!" I jumped, grasping at my heart.

Lois scoffed, "Great, you ask me out here and then act

like I'm a surprise. Who is this woman?" The ghost asked Meow as if he might answer.

He yawned.

"Lois, I'm so glad you came outside. Thank you," I said as the success of my terrible plan settled into my awareness.

"What other choice did I have?" She crossed her arms in front of her. "I'm naturally curious."

I observed her for a moment. Her brown hair bore streaks of gray, but she had it tucked into such a tight bun I swear it would've given her a headache had she still been alive. Her clothes were conservative, but the small, colorful brooch she wore on the pocket of her blouse gave me hope that she might have a less reserved side hidden away.

Literature was usually my standard for relating to people, and this situation was no different. Lois Butler seemed like a terrible mix of James's Aunt Spiker from before he found the peach and that awful Havisham woman who played around with Pip's heart. But there was also that brooch and a hint of quiet sadness behind her eyes akin to Beth March's character that gave me pause.

"Well?" She snapped in front of my face. "What do you need to talk to me about?"

"You're not surprised that I can see you?" I asked first. Asher's reaction to me had been so intense, so flabbergasted, it was odd to see this woman acting as if she talked to living people all the time.

"Honey," she said, placing a hand on her hip, "James Colin Gallagher and I chat all the time. You're not so special."

My head jerked back. "He can see ghosts too?"

This was amazing! I mean, he wasn't the friendliest person I'd met in town, but hearing there was another person out there like me made me feel so much better somehow.

Lois's countenance fell a little before she caught it and schooled it into a thin smile. "Well, he doesn't know we're having conversations … technically. The man talks to himself a lot, and ... well, I answer back." Her features sank. "Sometimes I forget he doesn't know I'm there."

Any excitement I felt fizzled like a candle after someone spat on the wick. "Oh …"

She pointed at me. "Listen, I still have a better chance with that man than your grandmother did." She said the word *grandmother* as if it were the name of a terrible flesh-eating disease.

I took a step back. "Whoa, I didn't even know my grandma wanted a chance with him. I thought they hated each other. Honestly, I came to ask if you'd heard what the fight they got in a couple of weeks ago was all about. He might have something to do with her death." I let the last part of the sentence out reluctantly, but who was I kidding? I needed her to have the whole truth, and who was she going to tell that I thought my grandma was murdered?

She flinched then bit at her cheek for a moment. "Like I would tell you anything that could get my James in trouble."

I leaned in close. "Meaning whatever they were fighting about was bad enough that you think he had something to do with Helen's death?"

She froze as she realized she'd given away too much.

Before I knew what had happened, she was gone.

22

"Oh, she's not getting away with that," I muttered, turning back in the direction of the doctor's house.

And I would've walked over there to find her if it weren't for running into another person. This one, however, was very alive and solid. I stumbled backward, blinking up at who I'd walked into.

"In a hurry?" Police Chief Clemenson asked, stepping back to steady himself from my collision.

"Uh—no, no hurry."

Still surprised by Lois possibly admitting the doctor had something to do with my grandma's death, my words were just about as unsteady as my feet at the moment. I glanced over at Doc Gallagher's house, trying to glimpse that slippery ghost, Lois.

Chief Clemenson followed my line of sight. He cleared his throat. "You've been here, outside Doc Gallagher's house for a while."

I scoffed. The man called the police on me? I saw him in the sliding glass door, ducking behind a curtain.

"He said you've been talking to yourself," Chief

Clemenson continued. "Thought you might've threatened him earlier, but in code?" The policeman crossed his arms over his chest as he said this part.

Ugh. The extent to which he was trying to get rid of me told me I definitely threatened the doctor in some way. Which meant he had something big to hide.

"Look, Chief Clemenson, I need you to listen to me." I turned my back on the doctor's blue house. "The doctor and my grandmother got in a huge fight the day she was killed. He called you to get me in trouble because he knows I'm close to figuring out what he did, and he wants you to look the other way."

The chief cocked his head. "Killed? Again with this? She died of a heart attack, young lady. As for looking the other way and distractions, I'm pretty sure you're making up this whole *someone killed my grandma* bit, so we won't look too closely into your connection with Frank Mastronardi."

I froze. "Wait … didn't my mother call? She was supposed to call you today."

He rubbed a hand across his chin. "Oh, she called all right, which only added more questions to my lists about you. We never take too much stock in the word of family members who love our suspects. They'll often say anything if they think it'll help. That and the fact that she called so many days after his body washed up seems a little convenient.

I felt like sinking onto the nearby bench in defeat. Mom's admission should've helped me, not hurt my case.

"I promise I didn't know him," I said quietly.

"I've worked this job too long to believe the promises of suspects, Miss Woodmere." He folded his arms in front of his large chest.

I groaned. I wasn't going to change his mind. I also

wasn't, at the moment, in handcuffs. Which meant that as much as Chief Clemenson thought I'd done this, he didn't have the evidence against me.

I shifted my gaze back to the doc's house and caught Lois peeking out at me through the window. I needed to talk to her more than ever. How was I supposed to get her out here now?

Glancing up at the police chief, something he said clicked in my brain. *I've worked this job too long …*

"Chief, did you know Lois Butler?" I asked.

He stared down at me for a second. "The one who used to live in that house?" he asked, gesturing to the blue house.

I nodded.

"Well, sure." He inclined his head.

"What happened to her?" I asked. Because under that tough cop exterior, the man was a small towner at heart, and I banked on him not only having information but wanting to share it.

He scratched his jaw. "Awful story, actually. It happened my first or second year at the station when I'd just come back from the academy. Her husband was very abusive. One night, we got a call from him saying she tripped and fell down the back porch steps."

We both gave the porch a once-over, perched on the large boulders making up that section of beach. I swallowed, knowing right away anyone tripping and falling on that wouldn't survive.

"Many people thought her husband pushed her, given his history of abuse, but as much as we could prove he'd hurt her in the past, we couldn't get enough evidence to pin the murder on him." The chief's shoulders sagged. "It didn't end up mattering though. He killed himself a month later."

I gawked at the house. "In there?" A shiver ran up and down my spine.

"No," the chief said flatly. "Desperation Cliff, out your way."

It was a sad story, but his association of me and that cliff made my teeth clench. When I looked back up, he was staring at me.

"Do me a favor, Miss Woodmere?" he said after a moment.

I wet my lips.

"Let your grandma rest in peace." He stuffed his notebook back into his front pocket, and he walked away.

Balling my hands into fists, I muttered. "That's what I'm trying to do."

And to do that, I needed to talk with Lois Butler. As much as I wanted to storm back up to the house and tell her what I thought of her attitude, the police chief's story had actually given me an idea.

If Lois's husband was abusive and possibly a killer, that must be why she's so attached to Doc Gallagher—her James, as she would say. He was a companion who would never tire of hearing her talk, never tell her to go away, and most importantly, never lay a hand on her.

But by living out her faux-domestic-bliss fantasies with Doc Gallagher, Lois wasn't moving on to the other side. I wasn't sure if she wanted to, but I was pretty sure I knew how to convince her to live her afterlife.

Facing the doctor's house once again, I noticed both him and Lois staring out at me from the sliding glass door. I tried to find something white to wave as a makeshift white flag. The only thing even resembling a flag was the thin cream-colored scarf I'd wrapped around my neck before leaving the house.

I pretended to walk away, hoping that would convince Doc Gallagher to go back to whatever he needed to be doing. Meow trotted next to me. I needed to get Lois's attention without getting more of Doc Gallagher's. I banked on the fact that she would stay at the window long after he left. The only person with more time on their hands than a retired person was a ghost.

Glancing over my shoulder, I smiled. My gamble had worked. Lois glared at me through the glass. I grabbed the end of my scarf and waved it in her direction, three long passes in front of my body. Then I turned and kept walking down to the next bench. As if he knew my destination, Meow raced forward and leaped onto the bench.

I'd just sat next to him, when Lois appeared on my other side, arms crossed.

"What?" she asked, her voice as clipped as her short kitten heels would've been on the concrete if she were alive.

"How about a trade?" I picked at a nail.

She studied me out of the corner of her eye. "For what?"

"You tell me what the fight was about between my grandma Helen and the doctor, and I'll tell you how you can find a man who will finally treat you the way you deserve."

The tendons in her neck tensed as she swallowed. "My husband was—"

"A jerk," I said, holding her gaze. "And most likely the reason you're dead."

Jaw tensing, she looked down at her lap, telling me she knew he'd killed her. Even though Asher said ghosts didn't remember the events that happened right around their death, Lois had been putting up with her husband for years, maybe even decades. She had to realize deep down that he'd done this to her.

Her unfinished business wasn't bringing him to justice; he'd done that himself. Lois needed to prove to herself she was worth being treated like a person. And as much as she seemed to love and admire him, Doc Gallagher would never be that for her.

Lois gave a clipped nod. "And where do you suppose I find a man like the one you're talking about?"

Meow jumped down off the bench to chase a fly. I leaned back and shoved my hands into my coat pockets, thinking about Max and how he'd smiled when he'd mentioned Lois. "He already exists. Well"—I tipped my head to one side—"exists in the same way you do. He's a ghost. He'll talk to you, listen, be a true companion."

I had more to say, but listing out those attributes reminded me too much of Asher and his friendship, what he'd become to me over a matter of days. Missing him had grown into a palpable ache in my chest.

The way she wrung her hands in her lap made me sure I'd gotten her attention, so I pushed a little further.

"What did they fight about, Lois?" I asked. "I get that they butted heads back when Doc Gallagher practiced medicine, but he'd been retired for over a year. What did they have to fight about now?"

I waited for her to talk. As I did, my mind spun, considering all the possibilities. Was it something to do with the mayoral election? Maybe Doc and Sam worked together.

Lois squeezed her eyes shut. I thought she'd lost interest when she finally spoke. "Your grandma came to him because she suspected there was a drug ring in Pebble Cove."

I coughed, flabbergasted. "What?"

Meow, done chasing the fly, rubbed up against my leg and meowed. Lois sat back and crossed her arms.

"Why the heck would she come to Gallagher about that?"

The way Lois's features tightened told me this was the part that didn't make him look so good. "He used to be an addict. Decades ago. Helen and I were the only two people who knew. She asked him to look into it, said he was the only one who would recognize the signs for sure. He wouldn't even hear more. He got so mad and kicked her out, telling her she was out of line for bringing that up, that she would be sorry she did."

"He said she'd be sorry?" I asked, shooing Meow away from my legs. I couldn't be distracted from the one clue I needed. Gallagher must've assumed she would tell someone and silenced her before she could.

Lois sat forward. "He was home that whole night. I promise you on my grave. He might've been mad at Helen, but he would never hurt her. Never."

The sincerity in her eyes made me want to believe her, but this woman also had professed her after-dying love for the man. She'd told me she would do anything to keep me from hurting him, so what would stop her from lying now?

Meow's pleas became low and throaty. I studied him but saw nothing that might explain what he was so upset about.

"He paced for hours," Lois said, and at first, I thought she was referring to the cat. When that didn't make sense, it quickly registered that she was still talking about Doc Gallagher. "I could tell he regretted how he reacted, that he was even thinking of going to talk to her, maybe apologize. But he did not leave the house." She left long pauses in between her last few words for emphasis.

We sat there in a heavy silence for a while. Well, except Meow. He kept howling and circling my ankles.

"Meow, knock it off. What's gotten into you?" I pulled

my feet under the bench and crossed my ankles as I thought about my end of this deal. "His name is Max," I said facing her.

"The cat?" she asked, gesturing toward the feline.

Meow sniffed as if unable to accept anyone wouldn't know of him. Obviously he'd become mayor after she died and being a stay-at-home ghost wife apparently hadn't afforded her the luxury of staying up to date on town happenings.

"No, the guy I told you about." Turning away from her as a couple walked by me. My neck felt warm as they stared at the crazy woman talking to herself.

I didn't know if I believed her story, but I could tell I wasn't going to get any more information out of her. We were done. It made sense to give her the information she wanted.

"He hangs out at the abandoned cannery." I checked to make sure the couple was out of earshot before turning to face her again. "Can you go there?"

She nodded.

"Don't tell me, you worked there when you were younger too?" Even with the foreboding doubt sitting on my chest after what I'd learned, I had to chuckle at the question.

"My first job." Her eyes sparkled. "Max, huh? I think I've met him."

"You have. And you made an impressio—" I clammed up as I noticed another person approaching my bench, hoping they hadn't heard me talking to myself.

When I recognized the person as the Rickster and heard him talking to himself, my shoulders dropped in relief. The Rickster gave me a salute as he passed and then continued to chatter away.

Chuckling, I turned my attention back to Lois. The light that had started in her eyes spread to the rest of her face.

"Thanks, Rosemary. I hope you find out what happened to your grandmother even if I didn't care too much for her when she was alive." She shot me an impish grin and disappeared.

"Okay. What is it, Meow?" I finally gave him my attention.

He glowered at me, and I swear a growl rumbled in his ghostly throat. Tail flicking twice, he gestured for me to follow him just as he had the other day.

"What is it now?" I asked, standing.

He took off down the street, and I had to jog to keep up with him. About to call out to stop him, I clamped my mouth shut as I realized where he was leading me.

Town hall.

Apart from the lighthouse and the old community church they kept as a historical landmark, the town hall building was Pebble Cove's pride and joy. And even though the exterior architecture and large columns matched the Victorian style of the town, the interior was modern and sleek.

Meow slipped in through the glass doors. I opened them, entering behind him, finding myself in an empty foyer with lists of the different offices inside. Meow trotted down a hallway, and I followed, wishing I'd worn less squeaky shoes as I tread across the polished tile floors.

The hallway we crept down forked, and Meow took a sharp left. I kept up, checking over my shoulder to make sure no one saw me. But when I glanced forward again, Meow was gone. I screeched to a stop. The noise from my sneakers bounced off the hallway walls in a deafening cacophony.

Wincing, I scanned the hallway for the cat I'd lost. He was behind me, having stopped at a doorway. "Mayor Sam Hoff" was printed in frosted lettering on the glass door. My heartbeat pulsed in my ears in anticipation.

Meow shot me a measured glare, waving his tail in two long arcs. Unsure what that meant, but positive the movement differed from his earlier "follow me" tail flicks, I waited. The cat took a tentative step forward, so the front half of his body stuck through the door. Backing up, he gave me those two "follow me" tail flicks again before disappearing inside. I opened the door. The office lobby was empty, and I slipped down another smaller hallway after Meow.

The sharp, spiced scent of the mayor's cologne pricked at my nostrils as I followed Meow to an office. The smell reminded me of my first day in town when he'd come to see me. The cat stopped in front of the open door. Unlike the bright reception area and hallway, the office lights were off, and the large room gave off an ominous air. I hoped that meant the mayor had left for the day.

Inside, a gargantuan desk loomed in the corner, looking suspiciously new. A vision of Sam yelling at a secretary to order him a *real man's* desk played all too easily in my mind. *But maybe there hadn't been a desk in here before*, I thought, trying to be fair. A cat mayor would've had no use for a desk, after all.

Nothing jumped out at me as to what was so important or wrong that would explain what Meow was losing his whiskers over. The cat's ghostly form skittered over to the bottom shelf of the bookcase in the back corner of the room. He scratched at the thick spine of a book. Gilt vertical lettering told me it was a collection of Charles Dickens's most famous works.

"A book?" I whispered to the cat, exasperated.

Pulling my sleeves forward so they covered my hands, I slid the book from its place on the shelf. I didn't want my prints to show up all over it if it was evidence.

Being a Dickens fan, I softened toward the mayor as I held it. Maybe I'd gotten him all wrong. I shot a pointed glare at the cat.

"Meow, inside this better be something good, like a note about how he killed my grandma being used as a bookmark."

Flipping open the front cover, I gasped.

23

The book didn't contain a written confession, but it might as well have. The large tome had been hollowed out, the remaining borders of the pages glued together so they created a hidden space.

The opening contained a plastic baggy full of white powder. As if this book knew everything I needed, it also held a single business card. I could read the name from where it was nestled inside:

Frank Mastronardi - LMH Property Development Inc.

I gasped as I surveyed the clues I'd been searching for.

"Meow, this is huge."

The large tabby moved in a serpentine pattern around me, jumping up and trying to rub his head against my hands that held the book.

"Thanks, former mayor." I wished I could pet the cat for real, but instead he continued to slink around me.

Grandma had not only been an obstacle in Sam Hoff's mayoral aspirations, but she must've also discovered he used drugs. When she'd tried to tell Doc Gallagher, to make sure she was right, the man had kicked her out before she could explain what she'd found. He must've been too blinded by his paranoia that she might use his past against him to listen.

It looked as if Lois told the truth when she'd said Doc Gallagher hadn't hurt my grandma. Sam Hoff was the killer, and I held proof he'd also known Frank. My thoughts flashed back to the day Asher and I had found Frank's body, to the mayor's odd visit. He'd said he wanted to welcome me to town, but in actuality he'd been worried that I'd talked to Frank, and I might connect the two of them. Why else would he care about that unless he knew he'd be implicated in his death?

Standing up, I froze. I needed Chief Clemenson to find this, but how could I convince him to search a random book on the mayor's shelf without explaining how I knew what would be inside. I couldn't very well put it back and leave though. I'd already lost evidence on the mayor before by doing that very thing, and this was too significant to lose.

"Meow, I so wish you could go grab the police chief for me so he could see this." I twisted, searching for the ghost, but he had disappeared. "Meow?" I called into the dark room.

The light flicked on. For a stupid moment, I wondered if the ghost cat had turned it on. That was when I caught sight of Sam Hoff standing in the doorway, wearing a suit and a frown. His eyes were wild, scary in a way that made a shiver dance down my spine.

"What are you doing here?" he asked, his voice rougher than the sandy beach. But that was before he recognized the book in my hands. His nostrils flared, and his bloodshot eyes narrowed into a glare as they settled on the evidence I held. "Put that down!" His voice rose as his anger got the best of him. The mayor glanced over his shoulder.

Of course, he wouldn't want anyone to hear. If anyone

else saw this book and its contents, it would ruin him. A darkness came over his features that made my flight response kick in. I backed up a few steps but ran into the wall. The small office suddenly felt like a prison, one I was locked inside with a murderer.

"Give that to me." He edged forward, jaw clenching.

"I know what you've done, and it's only a matter of time before the whole town finds out," I said, steady and even as I retreated to keep myself out of his reach.

Placing the large desk in between us, I moved opposite of the mayor and eyed the open door behind me. He spotted my attention shift and reacted, moving in that direction so I had to back away from my exit.

I couldn't keep him at bay forever. The realization clawed at my neck in hot waves. Formulating a plan, I realized that if I threw the book at him, while holding on to the drugs, I might distract him enough to run toward the exit.

Before I could, footsteps pounded into the room. We both jumped.

"Mayor! Are you okay? I heard you yell, so I got Chief Clemenson."

A wide-eyed teen that had *intern* written all over his youthful face preceded a tight-jawed Police Chief Clemenson. I froze. The way the chief glared at me made me realize I might not be much better off with him than Sam.

"Oh, good. Arrest her, please, Raymond. I found her in here stealing things from my office." Sam Hoff pointed at me, teeth bared as he glared between me and the chief.

Pulling in a fortifying deep breath, I turned to address the chief. "I wasn't stealing. But I found something you'll want to see."

I expected Sam to lunge across the room as I opened the

book and revealed its secret compartment, so it surprised me when he simply crossed his arms and smirked.

Chief Clemenson's face paled as he saw the bag. The intern stepped back out of the room.

"She planted that," Sam scoffed. "I've never seen that before."

The chief glanced back at him but stepped forward, not supplying him with a response. Grabbing a tissue from the desk, he picked up the bag and peered inside the hollowed-out book at the card. His graying eyebrows jumped as he recognized the name.

"You knew Frank Mastronardi, Sam?" The chief turned to face the mayor.

He screwed up his face. "No. I already told you that. She must've planted that too." Sam ran the back of his hand across his nostrils.

The chief looked back at me, his brown eyes meeting mine before scanning my face as if he had mind-reading powers and was trying to take in every clue.

Standing straight, I squared my shoulders. "I didn't plant any of this," I hissed, just to him. "I found it here in his office."

At that last statement, the policeman's face tensed. "And how did you find your way in here?" he asked. "How did you know where to look?"

I gulped. I couldn't tell him the former cat mayor is now a ghost and led me to it. But without that information, there was no plausible explanation of how I got here.

"An anonymous tip?" Beads of sweat broke out on my forehead as my face burned with the lie.

The chief ran a hand through his salt and pepper hair and scowled at me like I might be the murderer. "I can't use evidence you found while breaking and entering," he said.

The frustration that had been on the edge of his tone now leaked into every word.

I narrowed my eyes at the mayor who swiped at his nose again. Then I realized what was wrong with his eyes. They'd looked wild and scary to me before, but that was because they were almost red, they were so bloodshot. Sam's pupils were tiny, his eyes shifty. Was he currently high on whatever that little baggy held?

The chief followed my gaze and his shoulders slumped. I was certain he noticed the same signs I had. "Sam," he said, taking a step toward the mayor, "are you taking this stuff?" The pain in his voice made my chest ache.

Sam's face grew almost as red as his bloodshot eyes. "You can't prove anything." He spat out the words.

Chief Clemenson flinched as if Sam had spit more than just words in his face. He shook his head, pulling his handcuffs off his belt. "You're going to have to come over to the station." He glowered back at me. "You too."

My momentary celebration was cut short by his addition. *Me too?*

"Raymond, you can't be serious." Sam Hoff glared at the police chief. "You've known me my whole life. Believe me, this woman is crazy. She was in here meowing when I found her. She's unstable," he pleaded, red eyes wild as he studied the chief's expression.

"Sam"—Chief Clemenson cocked an eyebrow at the mayor—"you have the right to remain silent, and I think you should use it."

Two and a half hours later, Police Chief Clemenson walked

into the room he left me in after he'd questioned me, rubbing a large hand over his weary face.

"So?" I asked. "Did you look into whether or not Sam has any ties to Frank's property development company?"

He nodded.

"And?"

He sighed. "And you're free to go." He held the door open and motioned for me to leave.

"Leave?" I let out a bark of incredulous laughter. "But what about Sam? Was he on drugs? Did he confess to trying to push the outlet mall on the town despite the knowledge that it would be bad for everyone except him? Did you find proof that he killed my grandmother and Frank Mastronardi because they found out about the drug ring he's running in town?"

The chief's fingers curled into a tense fist, and he let it fall against the doorframe "Miss Woodmere, it's not your concern anymore. We'll take it from here."

"Not my concern?" I slanted my body away from the chief. "My grandmother was murdered; a man washed up on my beach, and a car almost ran me over. I'm pretty sure this whole thing is '*still my concern*.'" I used angry air quotes around the last bit.

Slouching, he sat in the chair across from me. "Miss Woodmere, you have nothing to worry about anymore. Sam Hoff won't be a free man for a while. If you must know, I just observed a young man who I've known his whole life confess to a felony, and I don't feel like arguing with a nosy out-of-towner. I'm sure you can see yourself out."

My hand flew to my mouth. "He confessed?" Stomach flipping, I was unsure if I felt happy, sad, or confused. "He confessed to the murders?"

Chief Clemenson pinched the bridge of his nose. "There's no evidence of murder."

"But I—"

"Yes, you told me you know your grandmother was murdered, and yet you have no proof, and her body was already cremated, so we have nothing to investigate." Unlike Sam's, the chief's bloodshot eyes told stories of long nights and little sleep instead of drug use. "I'm sorry, but I'm not going to accuse a man of murder off your *hunch*."

"What about Frank?" I asked in a voice smaller than I hoped for. "You questioned me like I was a suspect. How could I be a suspect if he wasn't murdered?"

"He had drugs in his system. He most likely killed himself."

"And you don't see a connection between Sam's drugs and this random man he knew dying of drugs?"

"Sam said he didn't sell them, only bought them and used them himself. Plus the drugs in Frank's system differed from the ones we found on Sam." The chief swallowed, hard. "And that's all I'll discuss about this case with you. I have a mountain of paperwork to get done now, so please see yourself out."

This time, I did. I wandered out onto the street and started for my car. My feet seemed to float, like maybe I was a ghost in a way too. I'm sure I was pale, and I felt transparent the way people looked through me.

I drove home in a mental and literal fog. The low clouds slunk across the roadways, making the coastal city seem eerie and quiet. Back at the tea shop, I set down my purse and plopped onto the sofa.

"Asher, I don't know if you're still out there," I said, talking into the silence of the library as I pulled a blanket over my shoulders. "But we did it. I think we found Grandma's killer."

I shivered, wondering if her spirit would still move on if they arrested him, just not for the thing we wanted. The important part was that he would probably go to jail. Right? It was still justice. But if that were true, then why did the chief's comments sit in my gut like a lead brick?

Tucking my feet up under my body, I stared out at the foggy beach. I wished my friend were here, wished I could've helped my grandma more, and wished I knew what my future held.

24

Over the next few days, I wandered around the tea shop, flitting from room to room, barely speaking to anyone.

The only solace was Daphne showing up a few times with food and news from the city streets. Even Carl stopped by once to make sure I was okay. Althea came by the third day to check on me, bringing a beautiful salad from The Pines' kitchen.

"Sam's arraignment was today," Althea said from across the small tearoom table as we ate lunch. "His lawyers made a plea bargain and got him out of any jail time."

When my mouth opened in an indignant groan, Althea put a hand up to stop me.

"Oregon is changing how they deal with drug possession charges," she explained. "Sending them to jail usually only exacerbates the problem. Whenever possible, they're trying to use rehabilitation. I heard he's paying a hefty fine and has to check into a rehab facility, immediately. Oh, and he resigned as mayor."

Mustering as much of a nod as I could, my focus

wandered out the tearoom window next to our table, and I got lost in the undulating waves. I returned my attention to our lunch, and I used my fork to move salad around my plate. My appetite waned despite the appealing salad in front of me.

"But nothing about murder?" I asked, my voice sounding hoarse even though I'd barely talked to anyone in three days.

Althea's gaze dropped to her plate. "No." She speared a forkful of salad. "The council is setting up another special election for next week." Althea paused before she shoved the bite into her mouth and chewed. "One of former Mayor Meow's grand-kittens, Whiskers, is on the ballot. Everyone said she's showing great leadership potential."

I tried to appear excited or happy at the news, but ever since the chief had arrested Sam Hoff, there'd been a hollowness in my chest akin to the hollowed-out Dickens compilation he'd used as his hiding spot.

"Back to a four-legged mayor," I said before forcing myself to take a bite of the salad.

"Your grandmother would be so proud," Althea said as she sipped a tea and grinned.

I returned the gesture but didn't feel as happy as I should. Althea must've sensed that I needed some time to myself because she wrapped up the rest of the salad, put it in the fridge, and said she had to get back to The Pines for dinner prep. Walking her to the door, I waved and then went back to staring out the window.

About half an hour after she left, the bells on the front door jangled.

"I've got to learn to lock that thing," I muttered to myself.

Looking up, I expected Daphne to clomp in, but it was a man instead, a businessman, judging by his gray suit and expensive leather briefcase. He was in his fifties, I would guess, based on his silvering hair and wrinkled forehead. He kind of reminded me of Chief Clemenson a bit. Not so much in looks, but in how he held himself. Concern emanated from him, making me wonder how new his wrinkles were.

"Hi, there," I said.

I was about to add that we weren't open when he took a seat at a table by a window.

"Can I get a tea please?" He rubbed his hands over his face.

"Uh—"

His hardened demeanor softened. "Thanks, it's been a heck of a day."

I felt so bad for the guy; he looked so grateful that I didn't want to say no.

"What kind would you like?" I asked as I walked behind the tea bar and set the electric kettle boiling like Asher showed me.

"Anything hot with leaves. Your pick." He pulled out his phone and started scrolling.

Observing him for a moment, I ticked through the possibilities. He seemed stressed, so a blend with kava would be nice. I tapped my lips with my fingertips as I considered the licorice taste the root held the other day when I'd tried it. That would go well with the balancing power of lavender. Scanning the titles of Grandma's blends, I pulled out the Calm container and started brewing a cup for the man. I brought it over to him, and his shoulders relaxed as I set the cup in front of him.

"Thanks," he said as he handed me money. He shook his

head when I motioned toward the cash register to get him change. "Keep the change."

I smiled in thanks, tucking the bill into the apron I wore. He closed his eyes as he took his first sip.

I was about to give him space when he looked up and said, "Tea isn't the only reason I came in today. Is the owner here? I need to talk to her."

My chest constricted. The man must've caught my discomfort because he opened his mouth. He didn't seem to know what to say, so he closed it again.

"Helen is … she passed away three weeks ago as of yesterday." My voice cracked. "I'm her granddaughter, Rosemary."

The man cocked his head as if he didn't believe me. "What? I just saw her. She was …" His face adopted a far-off countenance and then it paled like he'd seen something he didn't like in that far-off place. "This is terrible. I'm worried I'm the reason Helen was killed."

His words stole all the breath from my lungs, and I coughed. I'd said nothing about her being killed, but he'd jumped to that conclusion. And then there was the part about him being responsible. I sank into the chair across from him.

"You think she was killed too?" The room swayed around me. I fought to stay focused on the man across from me.

"Wasn't she?" He leaned forward.

I swallowed. "Everyone in town assumes she died of a heart attack."

He ran the back of his knuckles over his chin. "They did an autopsy?"

Shame and guilt vied for positioning in my heart. "No. We were estranged, and I didn't find out she'd died until days after they'd already cremated her. She had heart disease and was eighty-nine, so no one questioned it."

"Except you." He held me with his kind eyes.

I nodded.

"Well, I agree with you. Something doesn't feel right. She tells me she's going to investigate a possible drug ring and then"—he stopped to count on his fingers—"less than four days later, she's dead." He cut the air with his hand. "That's too much of a coincidence."

"You asked her to look into the drug ring?" I stiffened where I sat.

He grimaced. "I mean, I had to go back to the city and I couldn't, so she said she would dig around and report back next time I made it down to visit." His eyes creased in an unforeseen pain. "Until now."

I contemplated the implications of his words. "You don't live around here? So how did you find out about the drugs?" My eyes widened. "Are you an investigator? Do you work for the FBI?"

"I'm an *investment*-gator." He chuckled. "Sorry, bad joke. I work in an investment firm up in Portland."

His goofy joke reminded me of the punny jokes my father used to tell, and I softened even more.

"I'm from Portland too," I said absently, my mind still reeling.

"Small world. But no," he added. "To answer your earlier question, I know about the drugs because of my godmother."

The fairy-tale loving, ghost-seeing part of me thought, *fairy godmother?*

Realizing I still had questions, he added, "My godmother is staying down here at The Pines Restorative Center to celebrate her retirement. Well, she retired four months ago. It was supposed to be two weeks at the most, but she says she's not coming home. Last time I visited, she was talking about selling her house and staying there indefinitely."

I shrugged. "It's wonderful up there."

"Yeah, but it's more than that." He cradled his head in his hands for a moment. "I know this will sound crazy, but I think Ruth, my godmother, is on drugs. That's why she wants to stay." He met my gaze with a pleading focus.

"What makes you say that?" I asked, schooling my expression, so I didn't appear as doubtful as I felt.

He puffed out his cheeks and exhaled. "A guy at my office got hooked on opioids last year after he had back surgery. He came to work for two weeks high before any of us figured it out. I mean, we saw signs; we just didn't know what they were signs of. And the way Ruth was acting last time I visited, it was exactly like that."

"So my grandma was going to look into it for you?" I shifted forward in my seat.

"Yeah, apparently she knew someone who'd been a doctor and an addict. She thought that person might be able to recognize the signs and tell us for sure before we jumped to any conclusions. But now, she's gone." The man stared into his tea and took another sip.

Doc Gallagher. The missing puzzle pieces clicked into place, and I formed a full picture. Well, almost full. Chief Clemenson had said Mayor Hoff was only buying his drugs not selling them. This could be the missing link to prove otherwise. This man's information could be my chance to convince the police to charge Sam with the murder of my grandmother.

Sometime over the last few days, I'd accepted that him only getting busted for the drugs wasn't enough. He needed to pay for what he'd done, not only to Grandma Helen, but to Frank Mastronardi as well.

Clasping my fingers in front of me on the table, I leaned forward. "Do you think Ruth would tell you who she was getting the drugs from?"

His body sagged. "She won't even see me since the last visit where I confronted her about it. I just came from there, and they told me she specifically asked not to see me, that I shouldn't be let in."

Determination coiled inside me. "Well, what if I go? She doesn't know me. Maybe I can get her to talk."

For the first time since he'd walked in the door, his face brightened. "Would you? That would be amazing." But after a quick second, the joy faded. "But I don't want to put you in the same danger I put Helen in."

I waved a hand in his direction. "I was almost run off the road the other day. Grandma must've been onto something with this drug ring, and they've already tried to deter me from finding out whatever she was close to discovering. Plus one of the main players is out of the picture, so maybe we'll be okay now."

The man formed a steeple with his hands and brought it to his lips. "I don't know. It's too dangerous." After a moment, he glanced back to me. "You're sure this person who's out of the picture was the one who hurt her? I would hate to put you in danger too."

I nodded, feeling Sam's guilt as sure as I felt the wooden floor under my feet.

"Okay, then." He smiled, and his arms jerked up an inch like he wanted to hug me but thought better of it and downed the rest of his tea instead. Wincing at its heat, he stood. I followed the action, grabbing the empty mug from the table.

"What's your name?" I asked as he turned to leave. "So I can talk to Ruth if I see her?"

"Lance Howe, her godson. I'm her late best friend, Carol's son." He wrangled a wallet out of his pants pocket. Sliding out a business card, he handed it to me. "Ruth has always been there for me. Ever since my mom passed, the woman has become like my second mother. This kind of behavior isn't like her."

My fingers closed around the business card. "Got it, Lance. I'll go see what I can find out. The owner is a friend. I'm sure she'll help me sort this out."

He waved but paused before leaving. "I know you said your grandma and you were estranged, but … you remind me a lot of her." He tipped his head toward the empty tea cup in my other hand. "You even made me the exact kind of tea she did when I told you both to bring me whatever."

An ache spread through my chest, but besides being painful and full of longing, it was also warm. I was glad I'd come back to Pebble Cove, that I'd learned more about the woman I'd sworn never to speak to again.

As Lance left, I vowed to never let things go unresolved in my life again. People could leave you at any moment. Asher's absence still cut me to my core. And I realized it would've been so much better to have told him the truth. I thought I was trying to protect him, but I'd only hurt him.

Climbing into my car to head up to The Pines, I vowed to myself that if I ever saw him again, I would be honest.

25

When Althea had left after our lunch earlier that day, she'd said she needed to get back for dinner prep. I found her in the kitchen, chopping vegetables and chatting with a stocky woman about twice my age.

The creaky wood floors of the farmhouse held their own conversation as I entered the room, breathing in the mixture of garlic, whatever roasted in the oven, and fresh-cut vegetables.

"Hi, Rosemary." Althea's smile lit up her whole face. "Are you going to join us for dinner? Or use the sauna." She glanced outside. "There's still enough light left for you to walk the labyrinth."

I bared my teeth in an apology. "I don't think so, but thank you for the offer. I'm here for some information, if you can help me."

"Sure," Althea said, gesturing to a stool across the stainless steel table from her.

As I sat, I felt the phone in my purse buzz with a call. A peek at the screen confirmed it was my mom. With all my revelations about people I loved being gone in the blink of an eye, I wanted to talk to her more than ever. But this wasn't the time. I would call her as soon as I was done with this.

Silencing the call, I turned my focus back to Althea. "I'm wondering about one of your residents … patients?" I wrinkled my nose, not sure what to call them.

Althea raised her eyebrows with interest, nodding for me to continue as she chopped.

"You have a guest named Ruth staying here." My fingers tapped out my excess energy on the table. "I met with her godson. He's worried about her."

Althea's expression dropped like a raw egg onto the tile floor of the kitchen. "I know. It's such an awful situation. We can't get her to talk to him. I'm not sure what happened between them."

"It's so sad, especially because she doesn't have any family. He seems to be all she has left," the cook said, picking a wilted leaf of lettuce out of a bowl and tossing it into a bowl of compost scraps.

I chewed at my lip as I listened. Darn. I had hoped this Ruth lady would've at least opened up to Althea or some of the other people who worked at The Pines, since it sounded like she loved it here so much.

"Do you think she might talk to me?" I asked timidly.

Althea's warm face wrinkled in concern. "I'm so sorry, Rosemary. Probably not. And I get a little protective of people's need to relax and heal out here, so I wouldn't want to force it. Ruth has made a lot of progress here. If she doesn't want to talk to him, it must be because he's triggering feelings she knows are bad for her."

A lot of progress, I digested Althea's words for a moment. That didn't sound like a woman showing signs of illegal drug use. Doubt curled in my chest. Maybe Lance was wrong; maybe he was triggering bad feelings for Ruth. It was so hard to picture kind and concerned Lance as a person who triggered bad feelings. He seemed so close with her.

"Okay, well I guess it was worth a try." I was about to stand when something caught my eye on the ground under the stove. A small blue button. Located where it was, it would only be visible to someone sitting in my position.

A vague memory stirred in my brain. I'd seen a button like this before, but I couldn't quite place it.

Althea and the cook paused, concern stopping them both in their dinner prep.

"Are you sure you're okay, Rosemary?" Althea asked, placing her knife on the table and moving around to sit next to me. "Is there anything else?"

Standing to leave, I pulled Althea into a hug. "No, I'm sorry. I was lost in thought for a moment. I'll let you get back to your cooking." With a wave goodbye to Althea and the cook, I headed for my car.

On the way home, I returned my mom's call.

"Hey, Mom. What's up?" I navigated my car down the winding road that descended the cliff side.

"I wanted to call and let you know I've been reading Helen's journal, like you asked. I also read the letter she left me." Mom's tone was quiet, tentative, but there was a lightness sitting on the edges that gave me hope.

My breath caught in my throat at the news, and I pulled my car off onto the wide gravel shoulder right next to the cliff's edge. Through a few sparse pines, the ocean was visible hundreds of feet below. Putting the car in park, I turned off the engine so I could hear her better.

"And?" was all I could croak out.

She exhaled. "You were right, honey. I'm glad I did. She

wrote about us a lot, mostly you. I can see how much she regretted what she said." Mom's voice tightened at the end, and she added, "Probably as much as I regret not reaching out to her before she passed."

Warmth rushed through me. "Oh, Mom. I'm so glad you feel that way. Thank you. Hearing this is just the boost I needed after today."

"Why? What happened today?" Mom's words sped up with concern. "Is it more about that Frank guy?"

As Mom said his name, my memory zoomed in on the picture of him lying on the beach, of his blue shirt with those bright blue buttons, like I'd never seen before, except today under the stove at The Pines just now. His shirt had been missing a few of them.

My mind whirred with ideas as I remembered Police Chief Clemenson telling me Frank had reservations at The Pines but never checked in. But if he hadn't, how did his button get in the kitchen?

Unless … Althea lied.

"Rosemary," Mom said, pulling me back. "You there? Are you okay?"

I blinked. "Uh—yeah, Mom. Sorry. I just—realized something, but it doesn't make any sense."

"I have a few minutes, if you want to talk about it."

I explained to her the inconsistency between Althea telling the police Frank had never checked in and finding one of his unique buttons on her kitchen floor. "But Althea was Grandma's best friend." I shook my head. "I can't see her lying about something like that."

"Althea Pine?" Mom asked, a hint of surprise coating the name.

"Yeah. She's been kind to me since she was Grandma's closest friend here."

"That's odd." Mom paused, and I heard pages flipping in the background. "In her journal, Helen writes about how much she disliked Althea. She worked with her to provide tea for the restorative center, but she didn't trust the woman, not one bit."

My body flushed, making it feel as though all my blood had whooshed to my feet. "Wait. They weren't friends?"

"Not based on what Helen wrote in here," Mom confirmed.

"What dates are you reading entries from?" I asked, thinking she might be in an old section. People change. Maybe they'd only become friends recently.

"This was the week before she died."

The car seemed to spin around me.

"Mom, I need to call you back." I hung up and dialed Daphne before Mom even said a word.

"Hello, hello." Daphne's cheerful voice rang out from the other end of the line.

"Daphne, how did you know Grandma Helen and Althea were friends?" I asked, my words rushing together.

"Ummm … Althea told me, of course." Daphne's tone stayed bright even in her confusion. She didn't know the gut punch her words brought.

My stomach dropped.

Daphne continued. "Helen always visited The Pines."

I grimaced. That hadn't been because they'd been friends, it was because she supplied Althea with tea.

"Okay, thanks. Gotta go." I hung up. My fingers shook as I held my phone, unsure what to do next.

I thought about calling Chief Clemenson but remembered how he'd reacted when I'd told him my theory about Grandma being murdered. I knew the first question he would ask would be what proof I had. Lying about friendship and a button on the floor didn't prove anything.

Althea had no reason to hurt Grandma, or Frank, for that matter.

What if she'd lied about Frank so the police wouldn't be sniffing around The Pines? Police asking questions and searching for clues in a man's death didn't sound very relaxing at all. And she could've come up with the whole, "Helen and I were friends" story because she felt bad that my grandma didn't have family here to plan her funeral.

But other than the guilt that sat in my gut as I thought through that rationalization, there was also an odd wobbly feeling of doubt.

I looked up the road toward The Pines. The sun was dipping below the ocean, and I realized I needed to see for myself. Climbing out of my car, I locked it and started back up the hill by foot. Something in my bones told me I wouldn't find out the truth if she knew I was coming. For the last few yards, I snuck through the trees, knowing the kitchen looked out on the driveway and parking lot.

Branches cut at my face, hands, and arms. The forest blurred together in the gathering dark, making me squint to see as I maneuvered through the brush. The crashing sound of the ocean sounded to my left, like a distant friend yelling warnings I couldn't heed.

Finally, the glowing yellow light of the farmhouse cut through the tangled branches of the forest. I stayed low and flanked the house, glad now for the cover of darkness. The crescent moon above didn't provide much light at all. The darkness felt like a cloak of protection as I slid around the side of the house and peeked into a window.

The large dining room table was set, and an older gentleman wandered in, a book open in one hand. He read as he walked, settling into a chair without appearing to miss even one line.

A chime sound made me jump. It was loud enough to be heard throughout the house but still pleasant enough to be calming. After that, more guests filed into the dining room. Some chatted, while others sat quietly, smiling, and surveying the table.

My hammering heart slowed. These people were happy. Nothing was wrong here.

Scooting around the building, I moved so I could see inside the kitchen. Althea and the cook were working, just as they had been when I left them. A salad was going out to the guests first. Althea dressed it and garnished it with some sunflower seeds and a few ribboned carrots.

The cook put the final seasonings into a soup on the stove top before tasting it, nodding, and taking off her apron.

When Althea reentered to grab another few salads to take into the dining room, she waved at the cook.

"See you tomorrow," Althea said.

"Have a good night," the cook said as she grabbed her purse from a blue cabinet in the corner and headed out.

I slowly moved around the farmhouse so she wouldn't see me as she walked to her car. Once I heard the crunching of tires and saw her taillights as she drove away, I moved back to the kitchen window. I was feeling pretty silly for doubting Althea as she plated the soup.

I was about to leave, when she pulled out a small baggy of white powder, like I'd seen in Mayor Hoff's hollowed-out book.

Movements quick and eyes flicking up to the dining room door, Althea used a measuring spoon to place a small amount of the white powder in each serving of soup. She tucked the baggy into her apron and then stirred each bowl of soup until the powder dissolved.

If I hadn't been glued to the window, I would've stumbled backward out of surprise. As it was, the farmhouse whirled around me in my confusion, and I gripped the siding to steady myself.

What had just happened?

Was Althea drugging her residents?

I fumbled with my phone, turning on the video record feature as I held it up to the window. Any signs of the drugs were gone though. I was too late. She reached for two soup bowls and was about to carry them out to the dining room when her phone rang. Setting the bowls down, she answered with a huff.

"Hey, you forget something?" There was a pause as she listened on the other end. "Yeah, that sounds like her car. You sure she's not in it?"

Ice water flowed through my veins as I stood there, unable to move.

The cook must have seen my car. I was about to curse myself for not finding a better hiding spot, but I didn't have time. In that moment, Althea whipped around. Her eyes captured mine through the window.

Face clouding over, she ran over to the front door. "I'll be right back! Need to grab something from the garden," she called over her shoulder.

Panic flooded my thoughts, and I backed away. The door flew open as I ran toward the driveway. Althea didn't call out for me, which made fear skitter up and down my arms even more. She didn't want anyone inside to know I was here.

I'd only gotten a few yards away from the farmhouse when bright headlights flashed in front of me. I stumbled backward, hands raised to shield my eyes from the blinding light. Just like that night at my mailbox.

Spinning, I tried to look behind me, to run forward, to do anything to escape. Before I could ground myself in my surroundings, pain exploded from the back of my skull.

26

My head pulsed with pain as if it were being simultaneously squeezed in a vice and worked over by a jackhammer. I blinked, trying to gauge where I was, but the bright lights still blurred my vision.

A face came into my field of vision. I tried to focus, to see the person's features.

Icy blue eyes and a rough jaw came into focus, and I cried out in relief.

"Asher!" Tears pooled in my eyes. "You came back."

His face didn't display any of the excitement I experienced at our reunion, however. He regarded me with fear and worry. That was when I noticed that behind him, the sky was bright, almost white. I wasn't in the night-cloaked forest by The Pines farmhouse anymore. I was somewhere else entirely, on some kind of ghostly plane of existence.

Fear clutched at my esophagus, making it close up in terror. "Am I dead?" I asked in a hoarse whisper.

Asher frowned. "No, only knocked out." He disappeared for a moment, and then I heard him talking, but it didn't seem directed at me. "I can't go there. I never visited that house. It won't work. I need someone else." His tone was frantic, on the edge of breaking.

I attempted to sit up, tried to find where he'd gone. But before I could, a sensation like falling came over me and I jolted awake again.

This time it wasn't Asher staring down at me but that cook woman from Althea's kitchen. Her lips were set into a grim line. I became aware of the cold dirt floor of a barn beneath me and that she'd tied my arms and legs behind me. A gag that tasted like motor oil cut at the corners of my mouth.

The barn door creaked open. Althea rushed in, her eyes wide and wild. In her hand, she clutched a glass of water. "Okay, they're eating, so we've got about a half an hour." She pulled out a baggy from her apron, but instead of containing white powder like the other one, this one had two pills.

"You going to use both?" the cook asked her.

Althea frowned. "Helen only took one, but she had a weak heart. I think I'll use two just to be safe."

My whole body shook as I took in the words Althea had said. She didn't even acknowledge me as if I didn't matter. I squeezed my eyes shut, willing this to be a nightmare, but when I opened them again, the scene before me was equally terrifying.

The cook grimaced. "It would use your last. Don't you think we should save one?"

Now Althea glared at me. "If we do this right, she's the last person we'll have to worry about."

"You said she has a mother though." The cook stood and paced.

Althea rubbed the back of her neck as if this were just part of yet another long day. "Yeah," she said, "which means we'll need to make it very convincing that she killed herself. Maybe we should add a note?"

Chills raced down my spine.

The cook snapped her fingers. "That's even better. Save both your pills, and we can push her off the cliff. Then she won't have any drugs in her system, and nothing will point back to us."

"True. With Ruth's godson poking around about drugs, we need the least amount of connection to that as possible." Althea shot a pointed look at the other woman.

The cook shook her head. "I'm sorry. I did all the research. On paper and online, she had no family. How was I supposed to know about a random godson?"

"It's okay. We can't do anything about it now." Althea curled her lip. "I'm the one who drugged Frank without having him fill out his medical paperwork. If I'd known he had a heart condition, I would've started his dose even lower than we usually do."

Panic clawed at my chest as I listened to them put together the puzzle I'd spent the last few days trying to piece together. But it didn't feel satisfying, like it did when I was on the last few pieces of a puzzle. Here, there was no warmth of satisfaction or accomplishment. There was only dread. I was a loose end, and they were going to kill me, like they had Grandma, Frank, and who knows how many others.

I wriggled and tried to loosen one of my binds, but nothing moved.

Althea tucked the pills back in her pocket, resolute. "You stay here and watch her. I'm going inside to type up a suicide note. Good thing I know all about the fight she's having with her mother and the feelings of guilt she has about not getting back in touch with Helen. Those will be motives enough to jump."

"Make sure you draw Tyson's curtains when you're inside," the cook said.

Althea held up a finger. "Right, this is the only room with a view of the barn. Okay, I'll be back in a few."

The cook muttered something to herself about getting a different job and how she never should've let her talk her into this. I blinked rapidly, trying to remove a piece of dirt from my eye. The ground was damp to the touch and smelled like decay. We sat there in silence—mine forced, hers not, for what seemed like hours, but was only about ten minutes.

The thought of my mother reading a note about how I didn't want to live anymore left a metallic taste on my tongue that mingled with the motor oil. I wouldn't let that happen. Slowly working at the ropes around my wrists, I couldn't seem to get them to budge. Silent tears streamed down my face, settling into the dirt below.

As my body lay there, trapped in place, my mind planned. If I could kick and wiggle enough as they put me into the trunk of a car, I might escape their grasp. The only hope I had would be that small period when they would have to undo my ropes before pushing me over the cliff. They couldn't pretend I'd committed suicide when I was bound up. They would have to take these off before they pushed, and that was going to be my moment. My only moment.

While I was planning how to stay alive, the cook stood in the corner leaning against a stack of hay bales.

Until she wasn't.

A resounding *thunk* rang through the barn, and then there was a sound like a bag of potatoes hitting the ground. The gag in my mouth loosened.

I blinked the tears from my eyes and tried to see, but all I made out was a ghostly shape.

"Asher? Asher! Is that you?" I called, spitting out the fabric and rope.

My heart ached as his words from the white-space rang through my head, *I can't go there. I need someone else.* It wasn't him.

I squeezed my eyes shut and then open as I tried to free them of tears. After doing this three times, my vision cleared enough to see across the barn. I gasped as I recognized the ghostly shape.

"Grandma?" The word caught.

My focus landed on the large shovel on the ground next to the cook. Grandma must've used a burst of energy to knock her out.

"Shhh, shhhh. It's okay, Rosemary." Grandma rushed over to me.

Her long gray hair hung in a braid down her back, and her cheeks still looked rosy even though she was transparent. Like Asher, when he came to town, she was muted like tea that hadn't steeped long enough. I saw the energy she'd used to knock out the cook eating away at her. She dimmed more with each second.

She knelt next to me, and I felt her trying to loosen the ropes around my wrists.

"Grandma, I'm so sorry I didn't come see you," I said through tears as she worked. "I love you and I miss you."

"Oh, Rosemary. I'm sorry too. I've felt so awful for what I did, for years. I love you so much t—" But before she finished, the barn door swung open.

Althea strode inside, clutching a piece of paper in one hand and car keys in another. Grandma's face hardened, and her spirit flickered like a pulsing light bulb.

"What's going on here?" Althea gawked, her attention skipping from the unconscious cook on the ground to me, still bound but no longer gagged. "How'd you—?"

In that moment, a bale of hay flew across the room, straight into Althea. It knocked her off her feet and landed on top of her with a *thud*. Grandma's watery eyes met mine, and she began to disappear, just like Asher did after moving my car.

Tears ran down her cheeks. "Run, Rosie. Now," she said before vanishing.

Before she faded, the ropes around my wrists loosened a little more. Heart hammering, I squeezed my hands through the loosened rope. Out of the corner of my eye, I monitored Althea's unconscious body under the hay bale. A sob of relief pushed out of me as I brought my arms in front of my body and pushed myself up into a seated position. From there, I ripped at the knots tying my feet together.

The back of my head screamed with pain from where they'd hit me, but I pushed past it, standing as I kicked my feet free from the loosened ropes. Althea stirred with a groan as I ran out of the barn, turning left to run down the driveway and toward my car. I patted my pockets, searching for my keys and my phone. I needed to call the police.

My feet came to a sudden stop as I froze in the middle of the long driveway.

They'd taken both my phone and my keys.

The back of my neck went cold then hot, and another sob peeled out of me. I grimaced back at the barn then the farmhouse. Warm light spilled out of the windows in an oxymoronic lie. But there were people inside, and some of them had to have phones.

She couldn't kill all of us. Right? The thought was too terrifying to answer with any certainty, so I turned toward the farmhouse and scrambled up the steps. The front door was unlocked. I pushed through and slammed it behind me, throwing the lock.

Every bone in my body hoped Althea didn't have her house keys on the same ring as her car keys. I ran toward the back of the house and flipped that lock too. Then I raced into the dining room.

"Help," I panted as I pushed through the door and found a half-dozen people sitting around the table.

They blinked up at me. Some of their faces wrinkled in concern; some smiled lazily at me. Right. She'd drugged them.

"What can we do for you, young lady?" an older woman asked, rising slowly.

"Do any of you have phones?" I asked, racing forward.

They looked at each other and shook their heads.

"It's part of the relaxation. No digital distractions," a man said.

The same older woman held up a finger. "She took them when we checked in."

My thoughts raced in panicked roads toward a solution.

"Is there a phone here in the farmhouse?" I asked.

They glanced around, confused. "I don't think so," someone said.

"I need to call the police. We're all in danger." My attention flashed around the room, trying to see out the windows.

Were all the windows locked? What if there was another entrance I didn't know about? Althea was bound to get inside. She knew this house like the back of her hand, and I'd been here twice.

There was only one solution. "Where'd she put your phones?" I asked, focusing on the woman who seemed the most lucid.

She studied the ceiling for a moment. "I think they're in the cabinet in the kitchen. The blue one."

The same one I'd seen the cook grab her purse out of earlier. I raced into the kitchen and located the cabinet she was talking about. I pulled out each drawer and opened each door until I found a basket full of phones. Sticky notes taped to the front told which person each belonged to, but I didn't care. I ripped the notes off as I jammed at any button I could find, hoping to turn one on. After pressing all the buttons, I threw each phone on the counter and moved onto the next.

From where I stood, I had a clear view of the barn. The door swung on its hinges as if someone had just left. Terror raced through my veins, and I pawed at the buttons on the last few phones. But their screens remained black. They were all dead.

I swallowed. The word dead was all too real to me right now.

Fear spiked through my body as a digital sound trilled out. I jumped when one screen flashed to life. I almost cried. Pressing the buttons, realized it needed a code. I didn't have that. Nor did I know whose phone it was since I'd pulled off all the sticky notes.

About to run back into the dining room to see if anyone recognized the phone, the emergency bypass option flickered on the screen.

Yes! I thought as I pressed it and dialed 911.

But as I was telling the operator I was at The Pines, that Althea Pine was trying to kill me, and there were seven of us here in mortal danger, the front doorknob jiggled. Fear rolled into the room like a storm onto the coastline.

"Miss Woodmere?" the operator asked when I cut off in the middle of a sentence, fear freezing my throat.

"She's here," I whispered, tensed and ready to run. But the sound of the door opening didn't follow. Momentary relief flooded through me. She didn't have her key. "I've locked her out of the house, but I'm not sure if there's another way for her to get inside."

"I'm sending the police. Is there a basement?" the operator asked.

A chill washed over me. When I'd been sneaking around outside, I'd noticed small windows above the groundline. In an old house like this, it was possible there was a separate entrance to the basement.

"I think there is. Hold on." I raced from the kitchen and found three doors in the main entry hall.

One led to a small bathroom, another to a coat closet, but the one under the staircase held its own staircase leading down. My fingers scrambled, searching for a lock on the doorknob. Maybe if I locked it from here she wouldn't be able to come up. But there was none. I could block the door with something. I scanned the hallway, but only found a large wooden grandfather clock I was sure I wouldn't be able to move. I gulped. I would have to go down there.

"I'm going downstairs," I whispered to the woman on the phone.

She didn't need to know that, but I felt like if I didn't say it out loud, I wouldn't go through with it. A hanging light bulb in front of me lit my way down the stairs when I pulled the chain. I held my breath as I crept down one stair at a time. Each step creaked as my weight moved onto it, and I couldn't tell if the sounds reminded me more of warnings or threats.

Cold air swept up to meet me, smelling like roots and damp earth. The dim light was far behind me by the time I reached the bottom step, and I squinted to make out shapes in the basement's darkness. Boxes were stacked along one wall; there was a bench that held gardening supplies to my right, and straight ahead, there was a door.

It was an older-fashioned door and about half of it was made from diagonally cut windows. The part of my brain that is in charge of nightmares made me think I saw the outline of Althea's face in the pale glow of the outside light more than once.

I reached my shaking hand forward as I kept my eyes glued on the window, just in case that picture wasn't only in my mind. When my fingers closed over the knob, I turned it right, then left. All the breath left my lungs in a relieved exhale.

"It's locked," I told the operator.

But she didn't respond as she had before. I scrutinized the phone and realized it had died.

I was alone.

The sound of shattering glass rang out from upstairs. Footsteps creaked across the old wood floors. My instinct was to find somewhere down here in the basement to hide. But there were six innocent people upstairs. I couldn't leave them to Althea's mercy. Who knew what she might do at this point. I had to go up there and help them.

My fingers curled around a garden trowel hanging from a nail to my right. I spun around, pulling in deep breaths as if they might fill me with courage. Being armed, no matter how feebly, gave me the nerve to ascend the stairs. Heart-beat pounding in my chest, in my temples, in my eardrums, I no longer heard the complaints of the old stairs.

At the landing, I leaned close to the door, trying to pick up sounds of movement in the hallway. Light spilled in from the gap underneath. Footsteps stopped right outside, and before I could scramble back down, the door swung open.

"Rosemary," Police Chief Clemenson said in relief as I raised the trowel above my head. He caught my arm. I fell toward into him, sobs wracking my body. The trowel clattered to the floor as he held me tight. "It's okay. You're safe. Everyone's safe."

27

Mom wrapped her hands around the mug of tea in front of her and held on tight. I knew the gesture was more about the chill in the air than a love of tea, but I appreciated her for trying all the same.

She'd driven down the last night after I'd called her. With the combination of escaping Althea's wrath and having my mom's warm presence here, I'd fallen asleep the moment my head hit the pillow. Police Chief Clemenson had filled her in on some of what happened to me, but I still had a lot of explaining to do the next morning.

I was still in my head about having seen Asher and Grandma yesterday, and the questions piled up. Why had Grandma waited until that moment to show up? It sounded like he'd helped find her last night, helped bring her to me. If he could've done that, why had he waited? And even though I didn't expect to see her anytime soon—I'd seen her use a ton of energy saving me last night—why hadn't Asher come back?

Mom, not privy to my ghostly worries, was more focused on the facts of the case against Althea.

"So she killed Frank too?" she asked, staring out the tea shop window at the beach. Tears still hung in the corners of her eyes from when I'd described how Althea had switched Grandma Helen's normal medicine with a lethal dose of fentanyl.

Trying to turn off the running list of ghostly questions in my mind, I nodded. "Apparently, Frank checked into The Pines the night he was supposed to. Althea lied when she said he never showed. He came in late, however, and the other guests had already gone to bed for the evening. She heated him up some of what they'd had for dinner, inviting him to eat in the kitchen after she'd added a dose of the drug she was using in her guests' meals."

"And it was too much?" Mom asked, leaning forward.

I bit at my lip for a moment to steady my breath. "She fed him before having him fill out his medical survey. She'd researched him online and knew he didn't have any close family members. That was one of her checks to make sure no one would come looking for the person when they stayed with her for much longer than they originally planned. But because she didn't know he had a heart condition, the drugs gave him a heart attack, and he collapsed right there in her kitchen."

"Which is how his blue button ended up under the stove." Mom snapped her fingers as she connected that to something Police Chief Clemenson must've told her last night.

"Yup." I sipped at my tea, reveling in the cinnamon and cardamom flavors of Grandma's Home blend.

I thought—for the seventh time that morning—about telling my mom about seeing Grandma's ghost yesterday, about how she saved me. But just like every other time the thought came to me, I shut it down. Mom had a hard enough time accepting everything else that had happened. I didn't want to give her one more thing to worry about.

Instead, I said, "Frank was only supposed to stay for four days, so she knew if she wanted to get him hooked enough to stay, she needed to start fast. But that recklessness led to her arrest."

Mom wrinkled her forehead. "And she killed Frank after Helen died—sorry, after she killed Helen? I'm still coming to terms with that." Mom exhaled.

"Almost two weeks after. Grandma Helen had suspected Althea of sketchy behavior ever since she started selling teas to her. But once Lance Howe came by the shop a few weeks ago telling her his godmother seemed odd, she made the connection that Althea could be drugging her customers. Grandma also knew she needed more evidence. Althea knew Grandma was getting close, so she silenced her before she could tell anyone." Sadness sank over the room, suffocating and heavy, as if all the sand from the beach had been transported inside.

"But she did tell someone," Mom said, checking with me that she'd gotten that detail correct.

"Yes. Well, sort of. She tried to talk to Doc Gallagher, but he … wouldn't hear her out." It wasn't as if I wanted to keep secrets from my mom, but Doc Gallagher's past with drugs didn't seem like mine to share.

Mom's fingers traced the handle of the mug in front of her as she thought. "I still don't understand why she drugged those people in the first place."

I'd wondered the same thing. Apparently, the cook woman who'd been willing to help Althea fake my suicide and assisted in the killing and drugging of others had developed a conscience. She'd spilled everything to Chief Clemenson when he'd taken her in for questioning, swearing she only looked the other way, that she hadn't drugged or killed anyone. The fact that she'd also been the one who'd tried to run me over that night by my mailbox—and had flashed the headlights at me last night that allowed Althea to hit me over the head—made me inclined not to believe her about the conscience part.

Chief Clemenson had answered almost all my questions last night after I'd given him my statement, seeing as how I'd almost died for the information.

I sat back, exhaling. "Well, I heard Chief Clemenson telling you about Althea's medical history, so you know about how it all started."

Mom nodded. "She misdiagnosed a young girl who wrote a book about the lasting negative effects of Dr. Pine's shortsightedness."

"Yes. And because she knew she'd never be respected in the medical field, she left it altogether. She bought the farmhouse property and started The Pines, still interested in helping people heal, just from a more holistic way this time." I sipped the last of my tea. "But business wasn't good. Pebble Cove isn't a tourist town, and people didn't want to come all the way out here. So she got desperate. She still had a contact in a hospital who could get her medications. The chief is launching a big investigation into that person's identity, since Althea won't give up the name. Anyway, she started drugging her guests with a small amount so they would feel euphoric while they were here. When they left, they felt like garbage. They went through withdrawals, but they didn't know that. They thought The Pines was the cure, and they needed to go back. People sold their houses, drained their retirement accounts, whatever they needed to do in order to stay."

"And their families didn't see any red flags?" Mom asked.

"They did. In the beginning, there were a few families who got suspicious and came digging around, so she began only taking guests who had no family, no one to check up on them. With Ruth, Lance was a godson, so Althea wouldn't have found him on any of her records."

"So then the mayor's crimes weren't related to any of this?" Mom asked, having heard the buzz in the station that Sam's court date was today.

I couldn't help the way my jaw clenched as I told her she'd heard correctly. "I mean, he was using an illegal drug, but his was heroin, not the medical grade opioids Althea used," I added. "And he had financial ties to the development company, landing him in a thick ethics violation. He invited Frank down here but panicked when the man showed up dead, wanting to make sure his name wasn't tied to him at all."

"Which is why he came to you asking around because he heard you might've talked to him." Mom put her head in her hands. "Instead, it was me."

I chuckled. "It's okay, Mom. You couldn't have known. You were trying to help me sell the house."

Mom looked up. "So …? Are you … going to sell it?"

I trailed a fingertip around the lip of my mug, wincing as I looked outside instead of at her.

A figure walking out on the beach stole my attention for a moment. My heartbeat kicked up a notch when I caught a glimmer of the ocean through the person. They were transparent, a ghost. But through my excitement, I recognized it was neither Asher nor my grandmother.

It was Lois.

Her hair was down, hanging in loose waves that

bounced around her shoulders instead of plastered to her head in that tight bun like when I'd seen her last. Then I realized she wasn't alone. Max walked by her side.

My heart felt light, and a smile tugged at the corners of my mouth. As happy as seeing Lois and Max made me, it also highlighted the ghosts I missed. I checked over my shoulder, scanning the room as I'd been in the habit of doing since Asher went missing, and last night when I'd seen both him and my grandma. But there had been no sign of either of them.

"You're staying, aren't you?" Mom asked quietly.

I nodded, keeping my gaze fixed on the beach.

She exhaled. "Well, other than you almost being killed out here, I have to admit that it seems like this place has been good for you."

My eyes flashed over to hers. "Really?"

She tucked a lock of dark hair behind her ear. "Really. You seem happy, more yourself than you have since"—her eyes crinkled at the edges, showing the pain it caused her to finish—"since we lost your dad."

A happiness surrounded me, almost as palpable as the relief I'd felt last night at seeing Chief Clemenson on the other side of the basement door. I hadn't realized how keeping my true feelings from my mother had been weighing down on me. I might not be telling her the *whole* truth—I couldn't see anything good coming from sharing my ghost-seeing abilities with her, at least not right now—but being honest with her about staying in Pebble Cove felt like a good start.

Telling the truth had its benefits, for sure. I thought about how I'd lied to Asher about doing research about him, the hurt written across his face as clearly as that article I'd read online. I hoped I got the chance to say I was sorry. But it was feeling like I would never see him again.

Mom told me she would stay for longer than just the weekend, but I insisted she get back to work. I would be up to the city soon anyway to move out of my apartment.

Watching her car pull away early that Monday morning, however, was much harder than I wanted to admit.

I puttered around the house, reading, cleaning, and thinking about how I might rearrange the furniture. I even left the front door unlocked in case Daphne wandered in to keep me company. And even though I hoped to see Asher, the sight of another man at my back porch brightened my smile around midday.

Carl stood facing the sea, hands shoved into his pockets, acting as if he hadn't just knocked on the door.

"Hi," I said, doing my best to disguise my happiness at seeing him, knowing it might chase the ornery man back to his hideaway.

He tipped his fisherman's cap forward and gestured inside. "Can I come in for a minute?"

I stepped aside. When Carl was inside, I closed the door against the chilly wind snapping through the flag on my porch. Carl sank into a chair right next to a picture window and stared out at the waves in silence for a beat before turning his dark brown eyes on me.

"Saw your mom left this morning." His voice was rough, like he hadn't spoken to anyone in a while.

"Yeah," I said, unable to keep the sadness I felt from coating every sound.

"But you're staying?" His eyes were bright with interest.

My heart sank. He was only here to see if I was sticking around, probably to try talking me out of reopening the tea shop. I studied my fingers, finding my nail beds easier to inspect than his face. "I am."

"Good. I'm glad."

Nails forgotten, my attention moved to him, studying for signs of sarcasm. "What?"

His mouth peeled into a grin. "I am." He chuckled.

I leaned closer to him. "And you know that means I'll reopen the tea shop, right?"

"I do."

Gesturing behind him, I pointed to the driveway. "And customers will come up and down the easement throughout the day."

He nodded then held up a hand to stop me. "I've been thinking ever since we had our talk that night in my kitchen. I was angry with your grandma. It was never about the tea shop. But if you can forgive her, I think maybe I can too. Or maybe the better lesson here is that I won't ever understand other people's relationships, and it's none of my darn business."

I swallowed as I took in his words. I hated that it had taken Grandma's death to make Carl realize he could forgive her. Then again, I was in the same glass boat, so I couldn't throw rocks … or fish, or whatever one throws on a boat.

A smiled edged its way onto my face, into my heart. "You're sure you're okay with it, then?"

"I'm sure." His bright expression faded, replaced by a stern focus. "On one condition though."

I raised my eyebrows, ready to hear it.

"You bring back the Fisherman's blend your grandma used to make. She stopped to spite me when we started fighting, but it was my favorite tea ever."

"Uh, sure …" I said. "I mean, I'll have to check through her recipes and see if she still has it, but I'm sure we can figure something out." The surprise that the solution could be as simple as that made me feel giddily dizzy.

Just then the doorbell jangled, and a pair of clogged feet clomped their way into the tearoom. I beamed. Leaving that door unlocked had, in fact, earned me a Daphne visit. I wondered for a second if she had a sixth sense for when it was left unlocked.

"Hi, doll," she said. "I saw your momma heading out earlier and thought you might want some company." She stopped short as she noticed Carl. "Oh! Hi, Carl." Her hand flew to her chest, and her mouth hung open. "I didn't realize you already had company."

I stood to retrieve another chair. Scooting it toward the table Carl occupied, I said, "Come join us. I was about to make some tea."

Daphne hesitated for a beat but then took her place next to Carl. As I rounded the tea bar to start the kettle boiling, I couldn't help but smile at my new neighbors.

Things would be okay. I wasn't alone.

The problem was, my days with Asher had shown me that not being alone wasn't enough anymore. I longed for my friend, for our conversations, for our time reading together, for the way he would place his hand over mine in support even though he knew I couldn't feel it.

He taught me to open up, to let people in again. I knew I wouldn't be here having tea with Daphne and Carl without Asher's influence in my life. And with all the uncertainty surrounding him in my mind, that was one lovely thing to be sure of: I was a better person for having met him.

28

It took me three days to move out of my apartment in Portland and into Grandma's house—sorry, *my* house. I was still getting used to that.

Regardless of visits from Daphne and Carl, missing Asher ate at me like a disease. So I opened the tea shop, officially, that next Wednesday.

Now that the news of my grandmother's murder and the attempt on my life had circulated through Pebble Cove, I was even more of a celebrity in town than I had been before. And now that they'd learned I was staying, any whispers of that city girl were quelled and replaced by talk of how great it was to have *more young blood* in the place. Which was much creepier than I'd hoped for in a greeting, but one I still accepted.

The teahouse's grand reopening was a blur, one I can only pick out flashes from. A smile here, a laugh there, many mugs of steaming tea, people sitting around reading, chatting, and filling my heart with hope. I only mixed up three orders, crashed the new computer system I'd bought twice, and burnt myself once—well, only one of my burns will scar, let's say that.

At the end of the day, I was about to sit down to my own cup of tea. Standing behind the bar, I ran my eyes over the different teas Grandma had in stock. I'd found a stack of her recipes in a desk drawer but was sure there had to be more around.

I made myself a quick note to contact her suppliers and inform them I'd taken over. In the meantime, I needed to become better versed in the tea we had carried. A few customers had asked questions today that I wasn't sure how to answer, and I didn't want that to happen again if I could help it.

"Let's see," I said aloud as I searched through the options. "How about you, matcha powder?" It was the thing that puzzled me most on the shelves.

I plucked the bag from the shelf under the bar where Grandma kept bags to sell, leaving pretty mason jars for display on the wall behind the bar. Flipping the bag over, I read the description on the back.

"Oh," I said as I scanned the text. "You're just green tea leaves crushed into a powder. 'It is special in two aspects of farming and processing: the green-tea plants for matcha are shade grown for three to four weeks before harvest, and they remove the stems and veins during processing,'" I read from the bag. "'Best served as a latte with warm milk and a hint of sugar or honey.'"

Pressing my lips forward, I said, "Let's give this a try."

I took the bag into the kitchen and warmed some milk, adding a little sugar while it heated in a saucepan. When it was hot enough, I added the recommended scoops of the green powder, whisking until it had dissolved into the milk. Pouring the mixture into a mug, I returned the bag to the tearoom. The mug was still hot to the touch, so I set it on the bar as I squatted to replace the bag onto the shelf.

"What in the world is that green concoction you're consuming?" a man asked, making me jump.

Oh gosh, I left the front door unlocked after business hours. Again. I worried for a moment … until I recognized the voice. Happiness coiled up inside me.

"It's matcha." I pulled myself up, standing behind the counter, and my eyes met icy blue ones I'd gotten to know so well.

Asher stood in front of the bar as solid as he was the first day we met.

"You're back!" I squealed and ran around, stopping short before I reached him. Wrinkling my nose, I realized I wanted to try hugging him, even if I knew it wouldn't work.

I lunged forward, arms wide. My eyes closed in anticipation, and I brought my arms together, hoping with all my might I would feel him.

But my arms closed in on themselves and the only body I felt was my own. I peeled open one eye at a time then turned around.

Asher was chuckling at me. "It was a nice gesture."

"You couldn't feel a thing?" I asked, forehead wrinkled.

He squinted. "Will it make you feel better if I say yes?"

I laughed. "Maybe."

"Then, yes. Now tell me about this green liquid you're about to consume. Please don't tell me you're so bereft without me that you've decided to end it all with a mug of poison." He glared over at the offending cup. "Or pond scum." His mouth dipped into a disgusted frown.

"It's called matcha," I scoffed. "And it's very high in antioxidants and caffeine."

I grabbed my mug, testing the sides to see if it was cool

enough to drink. Determining that it was, I put the mug to my lips and took a small sip. My eyes widened.

Sure there was an earthy, leafy flavor, but the creaminess of the milk balanced with the sweetness of the sugar made it coat my mouth like a dessert.

"Okay, I'm guessing by your face that it's good." Asher folded his arms over his chest.

"So good. I'm going to make everyone try this tomorrow."

Asher's face lit up. "So you opened the place," he said, surveying the dirty mugs I had yet to clean up after the last rush of the day.

I nodded, smiling.

"And you're staying?"

I nodded bigger, smiled bigger.

Asher's face pulled into grin wider than the lineup of locals had been long that morning at my grand reopening.

But my smile fell. "Ash, I'm so sorry about the other day, when I was supposed to research about how you—"

He held up a hand, stopping me. "It's in the past now. Please, don't worry about it. I shouldn't have gotten so worked up about nothing. You'll research when you have time. I trust you."

I clasped my mug tighter and took another sip of the matcha latte. I wanted to come clean about what I'd found out about him but not in the first few minutes after he came back. Plus maybe I could find out more, check the source to make sure it was true before telling him.

"I like that," he said, shoving his hands into his pockets.

I pointed to my mug. "The matcha?" I asked, wondering how he could know if he'd never tasted it.

"No." He beamed. "You called me Ash. I like that nickname." He slid his hands in his pockets. "Just saying."

I swung my arms at my side for a second before gesturing toward the library. "Okay, Ash. Well, let's go sit and catch up. I have a lot to tell you."

Asher's face crinkled into a question. "You don't know?"

I stopped.

"I was there at the end. Well, sort of." He ran his fingers through his hair.

Mouth falling open, my mind returned to when I'd seen him in my unconscious state. I'd been in some different plane of existence. Was that where he went when he was "in a fog" as he called it?

"You sent my grandma to help me?"

Asher lifted his chin. "I was worried about you."

"Not mad?" I asked, glancing at him warily.

He shook his head. "Not mad. I'm sorry I reacted the way I did."

"I'm sorry too."

"I felt so stupid," he said, raking fingers through his hair. "I'd promised to keep you safe and then disappeared on you when you needed me the most."

Frowning, I took a step toward him. "Hey, you're the reason my grandma saved me." I squinted. "Care to fill me in on all that?" I asked with a chuckle.

He smiled and dipped his head in concession. "I wasn't at full strength yet, so I couldn't come back. I'd never been to the farmhouse or its barn, so I wouldn't have been able to manifest there. Your grandmother spent a lot of time there. I gave her the rest of my energy to go back and help you. She wanted to see you, had been trying to make the jump back to your plane of existence for days, but she didn't have the energy to do so just yet." He gave me a sheepish grin. "Giving her the energy I'd been collecting in the days since I moved your car depleted me again, which is why it's taken me so long to come back now."

My head tipped back as I filled in the remaining blanks about what had happened that night. "But how did you find her?" I asked, remembering he said it took him almost two years to return as a spirit, and it might take my grandma as long or longer. She'd reappeared only a month after her death.

"She was always with you, followed you everywhere. So I didn't have to look far."

The thought of Grandma being there with me through it all sent a warmth tingling through my arms and legs. "Does that mean I'll be able to see her soon?" I asked. "She used a lot of energy to attack Althea, but she should gain it back soon now, right?"

Even as I asked, I knew the answer. Asher's posture turned rigid.

He smiled sadly. "You solved her murder, and you forgave her. She no longer had unfinished business, so she passed over to the other side," he told me.

"That's so … sudden," I said, though thinking back to the moment she left me in the barn, it made more sense. The way she'd said she loved me, had fought for me, and the smile on her face before she'd settle into that final, forever kind of peace.

A tear trailed down my cheek, and Asher clenched his fingers as if he'd been about to wipe it away for me, remembering at the last second that he couldn't.

"It's okay," he said. "She knew you loved her too."

"I wish I could've hugged her, just one more time." I swiped at the tear before setting my hand on the counter to steady myself. "If wishes were fishes, she used to say that all the time."

Asher reached forward and placed his hand over mine. "We'd all cast nets," he finished the quote.

Again, even though I couldn't feel him, the gesture sent a warmth through my chest and out to the tips of my fingers. "Well, at least one of my wishes came true."

The corner of his mouth tipped up. "Me too."

It wasn't until that weekend that I made it back to the library in town. The tea shop had kept me busy during the day, and the information I needed to research was not safe to do around Asher.

The Loft called to me as I entered the small library, but I stayed on the ground floor, sitting in front of a computer. Taking my notes from the last time I was here, I typed in Asher's regiment and battalion number.

The same material came up as before, digging me deeper into the dejection I'd felt the first time I'd read it, the terrible finality of it all.

Deciding not to lose faith, I did what my mom told everyone to do when they researched at the library: "Confirm your information with at least three sources, if possible." I nodded as if she were coaching me in that moment.

First, I went back to the Shot at Dawn article I'd only half finished last time I was here, starting where I'd left off. In the very next section, a line jumped out at me.

"Not one American soldier was executed for cowardice."

My mind raced. So that meant Asher *hadn't* died by firing squad.

It went onto explain that while the United States tried soldiers for cowardice, they had never gone through with an execution. Which meant I needed to go back to researching Asher's unit to see what happened to him after he was tried.

Searching again, I clicked on a different site, and then another. It was the third that brought me something new. This site listed the name of the officer that had been tried and removed from duty.

I sat bolt upright and blinked in disbelief at the name. It wasn't Asher Benson, the name listed was someone else. It hadn't been Asher after all!

Suddenly I felt terrible for ever doubting him. Excitement built in me at the realization that I could tell Asher what happened to him now. I just needed to find out what actually happened.

My fingers flew across the keys as I typed in his name and "World War I" along with his regiment number and battalion number. Then I tried it without the numbers, realizing he might've misremembered them after all this time. Nothing. Nothing came up at all. My elation ebbed into confusion. How was there no record of him? He was an officer in the army, for goodness' sake.

I bit at the inside of my cheek, remembering Asher's request that I look into old newspaper articles from Pebble Cove. After finding out I would have to pay for a profile to access any of the online newspaper databases, I asked the librarian if they had any records on file. I smiled in triumph as he led me to an old microfilm machine like we had in the back room of the library where Mom and I worked. I told him the dates I was looking for, and we found the relevant film.

Once he was sure I knew how to use the machine, he left me alone. My eyes ached as I squinted, moving closer to the screen the more editions I flipped through with no success. Finally, as my stomach grumbled in protest, and I thought

I'd have to give up the search, I caught the words "officer" and "Benson" on the screen. I stopped, eyes poring over the words hungrily.

But just as palpably as I'd felt the relief flow through me with the knowledge that he hadn't been the disgraced officer I'd read about, all of the terrible feelings came tumbling back … and more.

"Local Officer, Benson, Deserts Post."

My stomach dropped as I read through the article, explaining that he'd never returned to Fort Macy after a short leave, and the army had listed him as a deserter. The author of the article wrote about his own, and the town's, shock at this development, noting his good character:

"Though none of us know how we will react when courage is asked of us," wrote the author.

Head pulsing with a headache, I finished scanning the article, reading how, once they'd accepted the news, locals speculated he'd fled to Canada. Asher's family had moved away in disgrace.

I'd thought nothing could be worse than telling Asher they had removed him for dereliction of duty, but here it was. He hadn't even gotten to the battlefield. And although I'd come up with the new rule to be truthful and open with everyone, a pit formed in my stomach at the prospect of breaking this news to my friend.

My mind and heart fought with the words on the page. This couldn't be the truth. The internal scolding I'd given myself earlier at believing he'd been tried for cowardice burned in my memory. Was accepting this just as bad? Asher wasn't a coward. He'd talked at length about the honor of fighting for his country. Disbelief buzzed around me like charged air before a thunderstorm.

But then there was the article I'd read about the mental

and emotional strain on soldiers. Could it have proved too much for him and he'd decided to get out before it even began?

There was also his name, in bold print right in front of me, and the undeniable fact that his spirit had yet to cross over. Was it because he was a World War I deserter and his subconscious knew it? He'd said he understood the flight response that day I'd run out of the grocery store. Was this what he'd meant?

I hated not knowing the truth. Surely the army would've done an investigation into this. There had to be more out there than just this local article. Regardless, it was something I would have to look into at another time. I'd already been here for hours. The sun was setting, and the library would close soon. Packing up my notes, I headed out of the library.

"Hey," Asher said, appearing along with Meow as I walked down Cove Drive, clutching my secrets as tightly as my fingers gripped my notebook. "It got late, so I thought I'd come check to see how you were doing."

I swallowed as my gaze darted over to him. "Oh, I lost track of time. That library has to be one of my favorite places."

Asher furrowed his brow as he watched me. "You didn't check anything out?" He peered at my book-free arms.

"Finished the book I was reading, actually. No need to check it out." I laughed in a way I hoped didn't sound fake.

"Okay. Ready to go home? I hoped we might start a new book tonight."

This time I smiled for real, anticipating about how Asher and I would take turns with the different character voices as I turned the pages and he read over my shoulder.

"That sounds perfect." I glanced down at Meow. "I wish you could join us, buddy."

The ex-mayor flicked his ears and tail as if saying, *It's okay, I'm happy here.* In keeping with feline aloofness, he was an independent soul and didn't mind being on his own.

Before we left for home, I leaned down and said, "I hear Whiskers is doing a fantastic job as the new mayor."

At that, the big tabby looked up at me, and I swear he grinned.

NEXT IN THE SERIES:

Follow Rosemary and Asher as their story continues in the next installment of Pebble Cove Teahouse Mysteries …

Pebble Cove is home to more than just fishermen, Victorian houses, and coastal beauty. It also harbors long running feuds and buried secrets.

When a local man drops dead after drinking a matcha tea latte, Rosemary Woodmere suspects foul play. As a witness to the murder, she's called in for questioning.

At the station she meets a new ghost and learns the town's police force has a dark past when it comes to covering up murder. She might be off the hook, but can she let the case go when she fears the police might be repeating history?

To make things even more difficult, Rosemary's life with ghosts is getting complicated. While she searches for the truth about how Asher died, Rosemary attempts to help a local spirit encountering her own difficulties with her death. And while a little ghostly help might give Rosemary a leg up in this case, will it be enough when she comes face to face with the real killer?

ALSO BY ERYN SCOTT

Mystery:

The Pepper Brooks Cozy Mystery Series

The Stoneybrook Mysteries

Women's fiction:

The Beauty of Perhaps

Settling Up

The What's in a Name Series

In Her Way

Romantic comedy:

Meet Me in the Middle

HE AUTHOR

Eryn Scott lives in the Pacific Northwest with her husband, two cats, and a dog. She loves classic literature, musicals, knitting, and hiking. She writes cozy mysteries and women's fiction.

Join her newsletter to learn about new releases and sales!

www.erynscott.com